Cover photo ©2024 Hazel E. Baumgartner



Holoframe Publishing, LLC

8706 E 30th Ter.

Kansas City, Missouri, 64129 USA



ISBN 979-8-3304-9342-5

**This book is dedicated to my Papa, who taught me how to respect the wild, revere its creatures big and small, and safely and effectively wield a firearm.**

**This book is also dedicated to the memory of my childhood friend Daniel, with whom I spent many days in the woods.**

A warning to the reader: This book contains mature themes and subject material that may be disturbing or upsetting, including animal attacks, automobile wrecks, death, descriptions of human remains, dismemberment, foul language, gore, gun violence, and a missing child. I would not advise this book for anyone under the age of seventeen. Reader discretion is advised.

# Table of Contents

# THE WOODS

A Horror Novel

By Hazel E. Baumgartner

Edited By Makinzie Knox

# CHAPTER ONE

"I dreamed about her again."

Doctor Meyer looked up from her notepad at her patient. Thomas Carlini was a middling man in the most literal sense of the word - he was thirty-eight years old, the grandchild of immigrants from someplace in Europe, and was of average height and stature sporting a square jaw, short, black hair, and dull grey eyes. She probably passed a million men who looked like him on the street in her lifetime. If he wasn't her patient, she wouldn't give him a second thought.

"Harmony?" She asked.

Tom nodded, his eyes slowly tracing the cheap aluminum railing which segregated a grid of ancient, yellowed ceiling tiles above him as he laid back in his seat. "The same dream I've had a million times before. I'm there again, in Alaska. I'm walking through the woods on a foggy winter day. It's dark, there's snow out, it's absolutely frigid. I round a corner and there she is, just standing there in the trail with tears streaming down her face. Then, I wake up just like always."

Doctor Meyer noted the dream in her legal-pad, though admittedly Tom had indeed told her about this dream a hundred times before in the four years they'd been seeing each other. "You know you're still grieving, right Tom? It's natural."

"It's just, it's been thirty years, doc."

"It's an injury, one you'll have to carry for the rest of your life. Rest, therapy, and conditioning all help, but you're always going to have that limp. You've just gotta learn how to live with it."

"I know, I know," Tom sighed. His eyes retraced the ceiling tiles. Thirty-six. There were thirty-six ceiling tiles in the room. He had counted them hundreds of times before.

Doctor Meyer chewed the tip of her pencil in thought for a minute. "What about your brother?" She asked. "When's the last time you spoke to him?"

Tom sat up. "Jason? I don't know, maybe a month? We chat online sometimes, I guess."

"And you haven't seen him since…?"

"Last Christmas. Or two Christmases ago. When we went down to Texas."

"How is he?"

"He's well, I guess. He and Elise, they're doing okay for themselves."

"Do you ever talk to him about what happened?"

Tom shook his head. "He doesn't like bringing it up. Not after what all happened last time with Elise and them."

"Okay," she said. "We're about out of time, so listen. I'm gonna give you some homework. Talk to Jason. Make sure he's really doing okay. Can you do that for me?"

Tom sat up and nodded. "Sure, Doc. I can do that."

---

By the time Nathan Carlini pulled into the driveway of the little cabin in the woods outside of Juneau, Alaska, it had been nearly six hours since the tip had been called in. Nathan looked nearly identical to how his son would twenty years later, except he wore his hair much more tidily trimmed, a combover gelled into place to hide his receding hairline, and sported a sharp salt-and-pepper mustache cropped tightly along his upper lip. He pulled his rusty old blue pickup truck, definitely not the standard issue vehicle for the service but Nathan always preferred to use his own vehicle whenever possible, behind the two Sheriff's trucks and a black Cadillac he assumed belonged to the Federal Agent who had been called in. Before he could shut the door to his truck, he was greeted by the locals.

"Good time from Anchorage?" The sheriff asked, doing her best to make small talk. She was a stocky woman of six foot something, frizzy blonde hair greying around the edges and framing a face that was frozen into a perpetual scowl. The summer of 2002 had been a hot one, especially by Alaskan standards, and like every summer her skin had bronzed into rawhide, much like most of the white folk in the northernmost state who spent any time whatsoever outside under the midnight sun.

"Alright time," Nathan answered her question. "Most of the roads are intact this late into the season. Would've chartered a flight, but that's hard to do this time of year."

She extended her hand for a shake. "We're lucky to have you. Agent Maytag said you're the best in the business for this sort of thing."

"Well, I don't know about that," Nathan said, "but I know the best. Sheriff, I want to introduce you to my own sheriff."

The other door on the powder-blue pickup truck popped open, and another man hopped out. "Jesus Christ and good mother Mary!" The man said as he stretched himself to his full height, roughly six foot one if you included his boots and the crumpled brown ranchero hat he wore mashed atop his head.

"Sheriff, I want you to meet Sheriff Andrew Callahan of the Mat-Su Borough. Guarantee he's the guy for the job or your money back."

"Y'know," Callahan said as he rounded the hood of the pickup truck and stole the sheriff's handshake from Nathan, "I've tracked more bears than most folks have seen wild animals at all. If you need a bear found, I'm your man."

"Glad to hear it," the local brass responded. "Agent Maytag and my deputy are up at the house. Place serves as a summer home and weekend getaway-from-the-wife for a local guy, Walter London. He came up here for a fishing trip this weekend expecting to get out of trouble for a while, but found the place trashed. Suspected a breakin at first, but it's got all the telltale signs of a bear attack - forced entry, fridge turned inside out, and anything remotely edible missing."

"And you really think it's your problem bear?" Callahan asked, as he gestured towards the house. The trio started their way up the drive.

The sheriff nodded. "I'd hang my hat on it, yessir. Maytag talked to the neighbors already, they said they'd seen it in the neighborhood the night before. Said it came up above their car on all fours. Big sonuvabitch. Here we are."

They rounded a final line of scraggly fir hedging and came face to face with the front of the home. The metal security door over the front door had been bent nearly inwards, and a man in a green parka who Nathan recognized as Agent Maytag, US Parks And Wildlife, was collecting hair samples from the foam. He smiled when he saw Nathan, but barely took his eyes up from his work.

"Jee-sus Christ," Nathan muttered under his breath. The sheriff wasn't kidding. Beyond the forced-in front door, the house was in a state of disarray. The front door opened into an open great-room, which now hosted an overturned couch, scattered dining set, and a kitchenette with not a cabinet left unopened. The refrigerator had been ripped clean from the wall and knocked onto its side, where it had been open and ransacked. Food trash and liquid freon littered the kitchen floor. This was a classic bear move - to a bear, the sickly sweet smell of the freon in a refrigerator smells an awful lot like the formic acid in an ant nest, and ants are an excellent low-risk source of protein and an easy snack.

"Anyone hurt?" Callahan asked the question Nathan was also wondering.

"Not that was reported," the local sheriff replied, "but we're still pretty sure this was the same bear that mauled that camper out near Glacier Bay. Which means he's headed for the border. The Canadians have asked us to wrap up the job before he crosses into B.C.."

"Don't want an international incident," Callahan chuckled.

"If you ask me," Nathan mused, "it's more likely the Mounties don't have the balls to shoot a so-called helpless bear. Even if it is a killer." He turned to Callahan. "Go get Dingo," he said, "before the suit mops up all the scent."

"I heard that," retorted Maytag.

---

The little incandescent light over the stove buzzed softly, the only noise in the otherwise silent house. Tom had long since finished eating, and tucked himself into a recliner under the light of a floor lamp in the living room. His dinner tray discarded to the side, he now held a book in his hand, but was too deep in thought to actually read it. His eyes had wandered over the same page three times by now, but he hadn't actually absorbed any of the words, just looked at them.

*Make sure he's really okay,* Doctor Meyer's words bounced around in his head. *Talk to Jason.*

Tom sighed and set down his book and produced his cellphone from his pocket. 2:24 AM, the display flashed. *Shit it's late,* Tom thought. *Guess I'll call Jay tomorrow.*

Tom stood and crossed the living room of his little Kansas City four-square house, passing the windows with the curtains pulled tightly shut as they always were after dark, and double-checked that the front door was locked. He made his way around the perimeter of the house double-checking that each window was secured, but doing his best not to look out them. He always got the creeps looking out windows after dark. He double-checked the deadbolt on the back door, then flipped off the last of the lights and headed upstairs to bed.

"Tom?" His wife, Isabel asked in a sleepy voice as he entered the room. "For God's sake, Tom, what time is it?"

"About eleven thirty," Tom lied.

"Why are you just now coming to bed?"

"I'm sorry, Love, I was reading and lost track of time." He laid down in bed and, without giving his wife a second to question him, said "I love you, goodnight."

"I love you too," Isabel muttered as she drifted back off to sleep.

---

Tom had, of course, always been enamored with storytelling and books in general. As a child, he and his siblings made their mother read her little paperback copies of *The Chronicles Of Narnia* until the ink smudged off the page, the spines cracked, and the paper itself wore thin in the corners where Alice rubbed her thumbs on them to separate the pages. He had been born in Olympia, as had his older brother Jason. Alice had met their father, Nathaniel, there while she was working an unpaid internship in a low-level office for the Washington State government, and it took until after two children for them to get out of the state. Nathaniel had worked during that time cutting lumber to size in a department hardware store to pay his way through college, and both yearned to escape to someplace with a lower cost of living someday.

That break came in 1982. Nathaniel graduated with a degree in conservation, and accepted a position with the United States Department of Forestry working in natural resource management. It was his dream job, working outside all day and traveling the country, living and breathing in the outdoors. He was assigned to work in the Alaska mountains, and found the family a little parcel of land outside the village of Skitooa.

The funny thing about Skitooa, of course, is its name. It seems like it's meant to sound vaguely indigenous, and that's because it is. Skitooa was founded on the southern side of the Alaska Range during the Klondike Gold Rush in 1898. Located roughly an hour and a half north of Anchorage, the village consisted of a clump of some two hundred wooden buildings inhabited almost uniquely by white settlers. These settlers saw the neighboring towns all had names like Nenana, Koyukuk, and Takotna, and decided that they needed an indigenous sounding name too. The problem was that, rather than asking an indigenous person what a good name might be, somebody just made up the name "Skitooa", and it stuck. This was largely indicative of what the next hundred years would be like in Alaska.

The Carlini family parcel outside of Skitooa covered around one hundred acres, ranging from streams headed towards the mighty Susitna River to open prairies to rolling hills, terminating in the forested crags where the woods took off and ran out into miles upon miles of no-man's-land owned by either the federal government, the State of Alaska, or out-of-state logging companies that came in once a year and picked the forests clean of any wood ripe to harvest at the time. The parcel was so remote, in fact, that the next-door neighbor lived two miles away in Skitooa, which had a permanent population of only fifty-five people. It was in this veritable paradise that Nathan Carlini used the expertise he had developed while working in construction and hardware to pay his way through college that he constructed a little three bedroom cabin for the family, surrounded by a fenced off yard, a chicken coop, detached garage and workshed, and a crushed-rock driveway spanning out towards the doubletrack road that ran along the river to the south towards civilization. It was the Carlini family's own little slice of paradise.

## Chapter Two

"I need this cut to size," the old lady said.

Nathan didn't hear her through his earplugs, he just saw her mouth move. Quickly, he set down his drink, removed one earplug, and asked "Pardon?"

"This wood," she responded, holding up a pre-cut length of dowel rod about two feet long. "I need it cut to size."

Nathan shook his head. "I'm sorry, ma'am," he said, "the saw isn't really safe to use on anything less than four feet long."

"But this is too long," she groaned as her face contorted into a sour frown. "I need it cut to eighteen inches."

Nathan shook his head. "It's too short, ma'am. I can only make cuts on lengths longer than four feet."

She held the dowel rod out in front of her and closed one eye, as if she were trying to comprehend its existence. "This is about four feet," she responded.

"No, ma'am," Nathan said, "that's about two feet. It's too short."

"Don't you get short with me," The woman snapped back. "I am a paying customer."

"Technically not," Nathan snarked back under his breath.

"Excuse me?"

"Technically," he repeated, loud enough for her to hear, "you're only a customer when you buy something. Right now, you're just an angry old woman with a stick."

The woman's face turned red as her nostrils flared with anger. "That's it!" She exclaimed. "I want to speak with your supervisor, young man!"

Nathan shrugged. "Knock yourself out. Hey, Rick!" He called the store manager. "This lady needs help! I'm taking five."

From across the store, Rick nodded and headed over. Nathan smiled at the angry red lady and ducked away. He produced a pack of cigarettes from his pocket - a habit he had told Alice he planned to quit yet had by-and-large only managed to quit around her and his sons - and ducked out the store's back door.

It was a perfectly dreary March day outside, chilly but not so much that it could be called 'unseasonable' for the Pacific Northwest. There was no sun, and despite the fact that it wasn't later than one or two in the afternoon the thick clouds overhead had cast a dreary pallid sort of dusk over everything. Nathan struck the cigarette pack against his hands a few times to pack the tobacco, then drew a smoke from the box and raised it to his lips. His hand slipped down into his jacket pocket to fish out his lighter as his eyes wandered across the deserted alleyway behind the hardware store, settling on the dumpsters where a white plastic bag was fluttering in the wind.

Behind the dumpster, Nathan noticed motion. His hand stopped moving, curled around the lighter in his pocket, and he watched keenly as a yellow-colored tail wagged out from behind the dumpster. Nathan pulled the cigarette from his mouth and let out a gentle whistle. “Come here!” He called.

The tail retreated back behind the dumpster and in its place emerged the filthy head of a young puppy. Its eyes were narrow and beady, and glanced nervously in Nathan’s direction. Its ears were erect and pointed, though one was missing a significant portion. The dog had the overall appearance of a feral, wild animal, sizing up Nathan to decide whether or not he could provide its next meal.

Nathan dropped into a squat instinctively, trying to make himself look smaller and less threatening. "Come here, dog," he coaxed, "I won't hurt you."

The dog cocked its head in thought for a minute, then seemed to make up its mind that Nathan didn't pose a hazard. Slowly, it lowered its head and emerged from behind the dumpster, tail tucked between its legs and belly practically dragging on the ground, mimicking Nathan's non-threatening posture.

"Look at you," Nathan whispered, soothingly. "You're filthy, and look like you haven't eaten anything besides trash in weeks, but there's a handsome boy under there."

The dog approached him and sniffed his hand. "What a good boy," he praised the animal. "Yeah, lemme get some food in you and you'll shape right up into a fine dog, a good dog."

---

It didn't take Dingo long at all to pick up the bear's scent. He was in no way bred as a scent-dog, but he definitely had a good nose about him. As soon as he figured out what smells were “bear”, he was pointing, and Nathan and Andrew Callahan hardly had time to grab their tracking gear and their rifles before he was leading them off into the brush. Hopefully the bear hasn’t gone far, Nathan thought, but he was apprehensive to say the least about running into the big ugly fucker once he found it.

As far as Nathan knew, the London property extended for some miles back past the cabin, so he wasn’t too worried about trespassing. Plus, even if he did inadvertently wander onto someone else’s parcel, he had a badge and a gun and as far as he was concerned he was on official business. A problem bear wasn’t going to hunt itself.

“Doesn’t it make you a little sad?” he mused to Callahan. “A bear’s a beautiful creature, and here we are out for blood.”

“Beautiful creature, my ass,” Callahan replied. “A bear may be a beautiful creature, but a *problem* bear is, well, another bear altogether. Do you know, Nathan, where the word ‘bear’ comes from, etymologically speaking?”

Nathan shrugged. "Do I look like a fuckin' etymologist?"

"'Bear' comes from the proto-germanic language, the ancestor to basically all western European languages, including English," explained Callahan. "It comes from 'beorn', which means 'brown one'. The original word for 'bear' in proto-germanic has been lost to time, but probably more closely related to the latin word, 'ursus'. The pagans of prehistoric Europe treated all bears as monsters, akin to dragons and trolls. They saw their raw strength and attributed magickal powers to them. The theory is that by calling the animal by its proper name, 'ursus', you would summon one, so they used the euphemism 'the brown one' instead, and it stuck around longer than the animal's original name."

"They're not all monsters, though," said Nathan, suddenly very concerned with defending the unproblematic bears. "That's what makes the bad ones 'problem bears' and not just 'bears'."

"No, of course not. And now we use the Latin and Greek names for them, scientifically speaking. Now that we treat them like animals and not monsters, we call them *Ursus arctos* in scientific literature, literally 'bear bear'. It's their old names, demystified once again. But out here? In the woods?" Callahan gestured behind them and Nathan realized that they had now followed Dingo far enough into the woods that they could no longer see the cabin, the relative safety of their truck, or any immediate hope for backup behind them. "Out here in the woods, a bear is a bear."

---

July thirteenth, nineteen ninety-two was a monday. At six AM, it was sixty-two degrees out. Mr. Carlini had spent the weekend at home, but was headed off to work again that morning. He came into the boys' room, shaking them gently awake, with Harmony clinging off of him like a spider-monkey, even though she was getting too big for it. Jason was fifteen at this point and wasn't fond of hugs, but was still glad to get to see his dad before he left for the week. Tom was eleven, and hopped out of bed to sleepily embrace his father.

"I'll be back in a few days," Mr. Carlini said.

"Where are you off to, dad?" Tom asked. "Anywhere exciting?"

"Let's see," he scratched the salt-and-pepper stubble on his chin, "I'll be driving out west, into Nelchina. Then I'll be mostly working in glaciers, which are always nice."

"Will you take me to the glaciers, daddy?" Asked Harmony.

"Someday, sweetheart." Mr. Carlini started to put Harmony down. "I've gotta go though if I want to beat traffic."

"Can I come out and watch you leave?" Harmony asked. All the Carlini kids loved standing out in the driveway and watching Mr. Carlini's truck disappear over the hill down the gravel driveway towards the doubletrack dirt road that led to the highway. Sometimes, they would run down the little doubletrack dirt road after his truck as it disappeared into the forest, until their little legs gave out underneath them and they had to concede that they couldn't win a footrace against an automobile.

"I suppose," Mr. Carlini said, hiking Harmony back up. "You boys be good. Take care of your mom for me, alright Jason?" Jason nodded. "And Tom, do your chores. When I got home Friday, those poor chickens didn't have any water.

Be good. I don't need your mother calling me home from work early again. You know we need the money."

Tom nodded, and laid back down as Mr. Carlini carried Harmony outside. He set her down on the driveway, kissed her forehead, got into his truck, started it, and drove down the driveway towards the highway for another long stint of work, watching Harmony wave goodbye as she ran down the gravel driveway after him, stopping at the property line and turning back towards the house.

That was the last time anyone saw Harmony Carlini alive.

About two hours later, Jason and Tom got out of bed and made themselves breakfast, assuming Harmony was back asleep in her own room. Mrs. Carlini was still asleep, and the boys figured that if they kept it that way they could watch some cartoons before they were forced to do their morning chores. Harmony being asleep was a bonus, because it meant that they got to pick the cartoons. Their usual choice was G. I. Joe, played from an old VHS tape that Jason had gotten from a friend at church back in Washington, which had been played again and again until the plastic case was chipped in places and the tape was worn thin to where it would fuzz and make the television screen jump about. The tape put up a good fight though and kept working, and the boys loved nothing more than eating cereal and watching G. I. Joe together.

"Good morning, boys!" Mrs. Carlini's bright cheery voice startled Jason and Tom out of their cartoon trance.

"Morning, Mom!" replied Jason.

She emerged from the bedroom, already dressed for the day, and made her way to the kitchen where she set about preparing a pot of coffee. "Have you gotten your chores done yet, boys?"

"In a few minutes," Jason said. "We're almost through this episode."

Mrs. Carlini shook her head. "You've already seen it a dozen times, Jay."

Jason groaned and paused the show. "Fine. I'll clean the bathroom. I don't want to deal with the chickens today."

Tom sighed. Feeding the chickens wasn't that bad. It was the eggs that were sometimes the problem, sometimes coming out with flecks of chicken-shit on them and always so uncomfortably warm. "I'll get the eggs, I guess."

"And feed the birds," said Mrs. Carlini.

"And feed the birds." Tom pulled on his shoes and went outside.

When Tom came back inside, half a dozen fresh eggs bundled in his shirt for safekeeping, Jason was back on the couch watching G. I. Joe. Tom put the eggs in the kitchen and asked him, "Hey, where's mom?"

Jason didn't break from his cartoon. "She's gone out looking for Harmony. Said she must've been out playing in the woods."

"Oh," Tom said. "I didn't see her while I was out there. Of course, I didn't see Mom either. It's a big forest." Tom settled down into the couch next to Jason and quoted the show alongside him. "And knowing is half the battle!" The episode ended and Jason hopped up to rewind the tape for one more view, eager to put off his schoolwork for as long as possible, even if just for the same four G. I. Joe episodes they'd seen a million times before.

The boys had probably watched that tape twice more before they heard the sound of tires on the gravel driveway outside. They weren't expecting company, and they didn't know where their mom was, so they stayed put on the couch right up until they saw a large moustached man wearing a tan suit and cowboy hat peering in at them through the window. He was talking to someone, so they paused the show so they could hear. That's when they recognized Mrs. Carlini's voice. She was panicked, frantic, crying even. The man in tan, who they figured was a cop of some type, was trying to calm her down, while another man took notes in a notebook.

Jason and Tom quietly exited the house and waited on the front porch for a minute while they listened to the adults talking. The Sheriff was telling their mom "Now, now. Everything will be alright. When this kind of thing happens, though, the first twenty-four hours are the most important."

"It's t-true," the second man said, looking up from his notebook. "If s-she's only been gone f-for a few hours, s-she can't have gone far." He spoke with a slight stutter, but still managed to exude an air of confidence and officiality.

"Ninety percent of the time, ma'am, when this kind of thing happens they're just out playing in the woods someplace."

Mrs. Carlini looked the cop dead in the eyes. "It's my daughter," she said. "I have a right to be upset."

"Mom?" Jason interrupted, stepping between her and the officers, "what's happening?"

Mom looked surprised to see the boys, wiping tears away and feigning a smile, but the sheriff was calm and collected. "Jason and Thomas, I presume?"

"Yes," said Tom. "I'm Thomas." Not many people called him by the long form of his name. Jason simply nodded.

"Your sister Harmony," the officer said, "she's missing."

---

"Listen," Jason said, "All I'm saying is that there's no way we get an entire franchise of comic book movies. It just wouldn't work!"

Tom laughed. “That’s what you think. I love the Fantastic Four, and I think the movie is gonna be incredible when it comes out this summer!”

“Fat chance it comes out this summer,” Jason chuckled. “The director just quit. Said he’s gonna do a Scooby Doo movie.”

“Fuck,” Tom sighed into the phone with disappointment. “Damn thing’s probably not gonna come out for four more years then.”

“Good,” said Jason. “Maybe Bush’ll be out of office by then. We all know Gore won that election.”

“Hey, don’t blame me, I voted for Nader.”

“Fuck you,” Jason said, only half jokingly. The two shared a chuckle for a minute, then Jason sombered up a little. “Hey man, call mom. She’s worried about you.”

“I don’t know why,” said Tom. “I’m doing just fine. School’s going great, and rent in the midwest is way cheaper than up in Alaska.”

“Just call her!”

“Okay, fine,” Tom sighed, then glanced at his watch. “Oh shit, I gotta go, man. Talk to you later?”

"Yeah, yeah. Just call her!"

"Will do," Tom said, and he hung up his phone. It was five-thirty, and he had a hot date with this girl Isabel he'd just met at seven. He had to get ready. He rushed across his little apartment, shedding clothes as he went, and turned on the shower. After waiting a few seconds for the water to get hot, he hopped in, got himself nice and wet, and....

Tom's shower was cut short as soon as it had started by the sound of his phone ringing across the apartment. He swore quietly to himself, and turned the shower back off. Wrapping a towel around his waist, he hurried back across the apartment and picked the phone up right on the fourth ring. "This is Tom," he said.

"Thomas?" A woman's voice came through the phone, sounding sad, maybe even scared.

"Mom? I was about to call you. Is everything alright?"

"Thomas," she sobbed, "there's been an accident."

## Chapter Three

Fred Molina was a family man, the same as many family men before him. He worked hard for his family on an oil rig, and his job had moved him around quite a bit. At first, he left his family in San Antonio while he was away for months at a time, but that was no life. He missed the touch of his wife, the sound of his kids, and even the little family dog. Since the majority of his work was in Alaska, he made the decision to move his family up to the little village of Skitooa to be closer to him.

It wasn't easy moving from San Antonio, where the family's Mexican heritage wasn't uncommon at all and most of their neighbors were like them, to Alaska, where the Hispanic population was so small that it didn't even show up on the census. The Molinas left behind all of their family, their church, and their entire culture, but it was in search of a better life. His wife, Mari, was excited by the prospect of going from a homemaker to a homesteader, and the children liked the idea of homeschooling enough, so in 1990 they packed up their things and made the move to Skitooa.

Fred was gone for weeks at a time still, out working on his oil rigs, but was able to return home every other weekend or so. In the meantime, Mari ruled the roost at the Molina Homestead, and she liked it that way. It was during one such stint of Fred's absence that her two boys returned dripping wet from a long day at the swimming hole with the neighbors, the Carlinis, and were sent directly upstairs to wash up for dinner. After dinner, they lounged around in the living room watching television until Mari came back inside from tending to her chores, drew shut the large blackout curtains across the cabin's windows, and hurried the boys off to bed.

Laying in bed, the boys talked quietly to themselves about the day's adventures. Mari didn't mind too much what they did once they were in bed, as long as they were quiet. This particular night, she sat out in the living room watching TV, folding laundry, and enjoying a glass of wine when she heard a loud thud.

"Boys!" She called with an annoyed sigh. "Quiet, go to bed!"

"It wasn't us!" came the reply.

*Bullshit, it wasn't you,* she thought. She started to stand up when another thud rang through the cabin, this time on the roof.

It wasn't the boys.

Mari ran to the master bedroom and rooted through the closet, producing her husband's Mossberg twelve-gauge shotgun which he left with her in case of bears. She racked the pump-action defiantly as another object clattered onto the roof and rolled down. Nobody was going to fuck with her in her home.

Another rock thudded against the house, and another. Mari sat dreading escalation, clutching the shotgun in hand, but the escalation never came. Just rock after rock after rock, for what felt like an hour. Finally, she had had enough. Gathering all her courage, she stormed to the front door, threw it open, and fired a single shot into the air defiantly, then re-racked the shotgun single-handedly.

As the boom of the shotgun faded into echos, there was no sound in the forest. The barrage of rocks stopped. Mari waited for a moment, scanning the treeline for signs of movement, but saw none. The night was quiet.

When Fred got home and she told him about the attack, he was enraged. He would go on to quit his job and move the family back down to Texas. "Coming to Alaska was a mistake," he would say, as if it wasn't his idea in the first place. The boys and Mari were happy to leave.

---

As Dingo led the two men through the backwoods behind the London property, they subconsciously paid close attention to the dog's tail. At times, the dog's tail was alert and spry, wagging back and forth happily raised aloft above his haunches. Then, the men would talk merrily and joke between themselves. Then, the dog's tail would drop and stick straight out behind it, denoting focus and readiness to leap into fight-or-flight mode. Then, the men would become uneasy as well, clutching their rifles, holding themselves lower to the ground, and keeping a keener eye out in the dense coniferous forest around them.

The pair walked for several miles through the forest, led by the dog, and as they left the relative safety of their four-by-four back on the road behind them, their revelry and camaraderie waned off until they were fully submersed in the grim task at hand, regardless of the position of the dog's tail. Finally, Dingo stopped and pointed again, this time at the ground.

At the dog's feet was an indentation in the soft mud of the forest floor - close to two feet across, Nathan didn't even recognize it for what it was at first until Callahan was able to form his own shocking realization into something resembling a coherent sentence.

"That's a big fuckin' footprint."

"Yeah," Nathan said, lowering his rifle long enough to produce a cigarette from his shirt-pocket. "From a big fuckin' bear. Look at the claw-marks," he knelt and pointed at them with the tip of his cigarette - long curved indentations into the mud, water pooling in their wicked sharp recesses six inches under the surface. "We're definitely dealing with a grizzly."

Callahan knelt beside his partner, measuring the print against his own hand - his hands were fairly large and even then the footprint crossed at least four of his hand-spans. He mulled over the math in his head for a moment before saying, "thirteen, fourteen feet tall. Probably fifteen-hundred pounds, unless he's hungry." He turned to Nathan. "You tell me, you're the expert. Grizzly?"

Nathan scanned the forest ahead of them. "Biggest grizzly I've ever heard of, if so. Let's bag him." Nathan lit his cigarette, then stood up and patted Dingo on the rump before following him further into the woods.

Callahan stayed behind and measured the footprint again. Four, four-and-a-half hand-spans. He shook his head and shouldered his rifle as he rose to his feet. "I sure hope he isn't hungry."

Several more miles down the road, the men discovered bear droppings, further confirming that they were on the right path. Then, the trail which they were following spilled out onto a doubletrack logging road, which Callahan said the map showed led to a natural gas wellsite. That meant people, which to a problem-bear, meant food.

The gas well was seemingly abandoned, though Nathan knew it was more likely closed down for the off-season. It was expensive to drive manpower and supplies out into the most literal East Jesus Nowhere in the western hemisphere, and it was certainly much more expensive to do so during the winter. It would probably be a couple more weeks before the rig was brought back to life. Machinery hummed along quietly, shaking the ground and spouting the rotten-egg odor of diesel exhaust into the air, but out of the entire row of parking spaces on the near end of the complex only one was occupied by a bright red Jeep Wrangler.

The complex itself consisted of two pop-up camper buildings pushed parallel to each other with a wooden deck between them, forming an H-shape. In the northern mouth of the H was a portable sheet metal shed which served to house some sort of tools or equipment. The southern mouth of the H opened up into a dusty man-made forest clearing in the shape of a semicircle some hundred feet wide that housed a generator chugging away dutifully, two upright gas wells with torches lit brilliantly atop them, and a commercial dumpster with a thick chain holding the lid shut.

At this point, Dingo had stopped dead in his tracks and was sniffing the ground underneath him, where another massive bear-track was barely visible in the dusty pavement. Callahan noticed that his tail was no longer wagging. They had found their bear.

Nathan let Callahan take the lead as the two men clutched their rifles and walked up the ramp and towards one of the two trailers, the one with the word "office" printed in capital letters in peeling black vinyl stickers on the door. Nathan rapped on the door with his knuckles and called out cautiously, "Alaska Parks and Wildlife. Open up, please."

There was a crashing sound from the other trailer. Both men turned instinctively towards the noise as Dingo started barking short, alarmed barks.

The trailer door was wide open.

"Alaska Parks And Wildlife!" Nathan repeated himself, a little stronger and more assertively this time, as he drew his rifle, flipped on the light, and pointed it into the trailer. Again, there was a noise somewhere in the trailer, the sound of weight shifting on the composite-board foundation. A heavy, dreadful weight.

Dingo barked again, then backed up out of the door's way. The hair on the back of his neck stood up and he tucked his tail between his legs, making Nathan's skin crawl. It wasn't in Dingo's nature to back away from a fight. Not unless he had no chance of winning.

Nathan's breath came in short, rapid bursts, and he did everything he could to try and slow his heartbeat. Behind him, he heard Callahan crossing the wooden ramp, and he held up a single finger as if to say, *quiet! He'll hear you!* He was beginning to think that calling out the way he had was the wrong decision.

"Hello?" Callahan called, raising his flashlight into the open doorway. The power was still on in the trailer, but the lights in the main room were off and the only light came in through two shrouded windows and the door which the two men were standing in. There was another crash inside. Callahan lowered his flashlight and drew his rifle as well, chambering the first round. "You think it's our bear?" He asked Nathan under his breath.

"Has to be," Nathan responded, stepping into the dark trailer. "Look at this."

Nathan lowered his rifle and reached into his pocket. Producing a handkerchief, he picked a tuft of blonde-white hair out of the door-jam at just above eye level. "That's not grizzly hair. You ever see one that pale?"

"Grolar bear," Callahan nodded. "Hybrid. Unpredictable. Dangerous. That's why he's become our problem bear."

Nathan reached into his pocket again to produce a plastic zipper baggie. Should the bear get away, the hair would provide valuable DNA information at least.

The bear emerged from the bedquarters at the back of the trailer while both men's eyes were down, its muzzle bloodied from a fresh kill. Whoever had been here before, they were too late to save. Dingo barked and turned tail out of the trailer, and the sudden sound startled the bear, who roared a terrifying, bellowing roar. In the close quarters of the trailer it sounded like a freight train horn, or a bomb going off. Both men snapped back up and raised their guns, but Callahan only got two shots off before they were knocked back as the bear charged out of the trailer. Callahan was thrown clear of the deck entirely by the bear's weight, which hit him like a semi truck, and he felt a sharp, stabbing pain in his chest as his ribs collapsed into his lungs. His ears rang from the roar and the gunshots, and panicked he cried out for the dog, unsure of its whereabouts.

Out of the corner of his eye, he saw Nathan, still laying on the deck four feet above him, as the colossal white bear lifted itself to its full height - thirteen or fourteen feet tall - and brought itself down upon Nathan Carlini with a terrific roar. Nathan screamed, but it was cut short as his voice faded into a raspy, bloody gurgle, and the bear's white fur was suddenly stained red. The bear then picked up Nathan by the head and shook him three times, like a dog would shake a rabbit, and dropped his crumpled body off the deck as his head came off in its jaws. It turned to Callahan and reared itself to its full height again and let out another bellowing roar.

Callahan was frozen in terror the entire time he watched the bear maul Nathan, but seeing it turn its cold gaze on him was enough to break the trance. He realized he was still holding onto the stock of his rifle, though only barely, and he lifted it out of the mud. For a brief, fleeting second, the thought crossed his mind to turn it on himself - it would be a quick death and probably less painful than what this primordial monstrosity had planned for him - but he pushed the thought from his mind and pointed the rifle between himself and the bear, which was making its way now off the deck. Lining the rifle's sight up with the bear's bloody muzzle, he let out the battle cry he had been taught in the Army.

"DIE, MOTHERFUCKER! DIE!"

Callahan had been taught that the time it took to shout this phrase was the exact amount of time to hold down the trigger on an M-16 in order to fire off a burst of three shots, and therefore the perfect amount of time to engage a target, but the three shots that burst from his hunting rifle hardly seemed adequate to kill the rampaging beast before him, so Callahan held the trigger down as he repeated the three words like a prayer. Mother Mary, full of grace, die, motherfucker, die! Die, motherfucker, die! Die, motherfucker, die! As he emptied his magazine, the sound of the firearm, his own roar of pain, fear, and rage, and the bear's bellowing cries all blended together into an unholy cacophony. Orange fire burst from the muzzle of the rifle, mirrored eight feet above by splotches of scarlet blooming across the beast's blonde fur. Twenty shots in all burrowed themselves into the bear - roughly one for every eighty pounds of its weight.

The bear lurched forwards covered in blood - Nathan's and its own, and Callahan dropped the rifle and rolled out of its way, hardly believing that he wasn't dead. The beast collapsed on the ground where he had been laying, going limp as it fell, and laid silent and bleeding. Its rapid breathing slowed as it rolled its eyes towards the sky, and then, almost cartoonishly, it stuck its tongue out, breathed what sounded to Callahan like a heavy sigh, and died.

Rising unsteadily to his feet, Callahan staggered back up the deck to Nathan's side, but he knew what he was going to find before he even came close. Nathan lay posed like a ragdoll, with his legs and arms both tucked underneath his body. He no longer had a head - his neck terminated in a stump into a bloody mess with crushed bits of skull littering about. Most of his jaw was intact. His chest had been ripped open and what was left of his uniform was just tattered shreds of tan stained in sticky black blood, hardly concealing his intestines which had been dragged out of his body. He never stood a chance against the bear. Callahan collapsed next to his dead friend and vomited on himself, before remembering the dog.

"Dingo?" He called. "Dingo, where are you?"

Footsteps rounded the trailer, and Dingo appeared with his tail tucked between his legs. He approached Nathan's body cautiously and sniffed it, before laying down at his dead master's side. He was a good dog, but he simply didn't understand.

## `Chapter Four

"Thomas? Jason?" The man in the tan suit reached out his hand, somberly. "I'm Sheriff Callahan. Your mother called me about your sister." Jason shook Callahan's hand, but Tom made no effort to. Callahan's hand lingered outstretched for a minute, before he withdrew it and wiped it on his khakis. "Have you seen her this morning?"

"Yes sir," Jason said. "She came in with dad when he was about to leave for work. She went out with him to wave goodbye as he drove off."

The other man in a sheriff's uniform stood nearby, taking notes. He asked Jason, "What t-time would you s-say that was, s-son?"

Jason shrugged. "I don't know. Early. The sun wasn't hardly up yet. I reckon it was around five?" Tom nodded in agreement with his older brother.

Sheriff Callahan checked his watch and frowned. "That's four hours by now. She could've gotten pretty far." He turned to the other man and calmly said "Davis, would you radio the State Troopers and see if they can't spare us a few men? Maybe a kay-nine unit?" Davis nodded, turned, and headed back to their black and white Ford Explorer. Sheriff Callahan tracked him back to the squad car with his eyes, then turned back to the boys. “Did you ever hear Harmony come back in?”

“No, sir,” said Tom. “Tell you the truth, I went back to sleep after dad left.”

“I see,” Sheriff Callahan scratched his head. “Do you kids play in these woods a lot then?”

“Yes sir,” Tom said. “We’ve each got our own Kingdom in the woods. Except Harm’s is a Queendom, on account of her being a queen and not a king. Do you think she might be there?”

Sheriff Callahan stroked his mustache. “I suppose it’s worth checking. When Deputy Davis gets back, I’ll have you take him out there. Jason, do you know where else she might be?”

“Well,” Jason thought for a second, “there’s the swimming hole out back, but Harmony’s not a very strong swimmer. I doubt she’d go out there alone, especially when it’s as chilly as it was this morning.”

"We best go check," Callahan said. "While Thomas goes with Davis I'll head back there with you to look around. Sound good?"

"Yes, sir," said Jason. "Do you think Harmony's alright?"

Sheriff Callahan looked off towards the woods. "I hope so, son."

---

The phone trilled in Tom's ear three times before it was picked up. On the other end, in a busy corridor somewhere, his mother's caretaker picked up. "Elm Grove Assisted Living, Samuel speaking," he said.

"Hi, Samuel," said Tom quietly, "this is Tom Carlini. Is Alice available to talk?"

The doctor's voice took on an air of concern. "She's here, Tom," he said, "but I'm not sure if she'll talk. She's not been doing very good lately. Still, I'm sure she'll be happy to hear from you. Jason called a few days ago, but it's been quiet for her since. Please hold."

Tom waited patiently as, twenty-eight hundred miles away Samuel placed the phone on hold. He rose from his desk and briskly walked down the hall to Alice Carlini's room, where he gingerly knocked on the door. There was no noise inside. "Mrs. Carlini?" Samuel asked. Still, nothing. "Alice? It's Samuel." He quietly opened the door and stepped inside. The lights were off and the shades were drawn, the baby blue room with white Ikea furniture and calm, boring department store art on the walls dimly lit only by the light streaming in from the hallway. Mrs. Carlini lay in her bed on her side, an untouched glass of water and grilled ham and cheese sandwich sitting on the nightstand. "Alice?" Samuel repeated.

"Who is it?" Alice mumbled.

"Alice, it's Samuel," Sam whispered. "I have a call for you?"

Alice lifted herself slowly to a sitting position, her black-and-grey hair pulled back unceremoniously in an untidy bun, skin burnt by the sun and marred by decades of smiles, frowns, and scowls, her sullen grey eyes wandering up Samuel until they settled on his face, quizzically trying to focus on him. After a few seconds, they lit up with recognition. "Oh, I know you!" She said. "You're that nice man who brought me lunch yesterday."

"Yes, Alice," Samuel smiled patiently. "I brought you lunch today too, which you haven't touched." He gestured towards the uneaten sandwich on the table.

"Oh," Alice said, following his gesture with her eyes until they settled on the sandwich. "Well, thank you."

Samuel nodded as she took the sandwich and nibbled a small bite off of it, washing it down with a sip of her water. "Alice?" he said, "I have someone on the phone for you. Do you remember your son Tom?" Mrs. Carlini ripped off another bite of her sandwich and chewed thoughtfully for a minute before looking up at Samuel and nodding. "Tom is on the phone for you, Alice."

"Speaker." She said, before taking a large, sloppy sip of water.

Samuel smiled and pressed a button on the phone. "Tom?" He said, "I've got your mom here. You're on speakerphone."

"Hi, Tom," mumbled Alice.

"Mom! You're awake! Hi!" said Tom.

Alice set the glass down. "What time is it there, Tom?"

"I'm three hours ahead of you, mom. It's eight here. I just finished dinner."

"Oh," Alice mumbled. "It's still light out here. I'm having lunch."

Tom smiled. "It's good to hear from you, mom. Are you doing okay?"

"It's good to hear from you too, Tom. I'm doing okay," Alice said, almost repeating Tom's words exactly. "I miss Nathan."

Tom swallowed back a tear. "I know, mom. I miss him too. Are you feeling okay, though? Your doctor said you're forgetting things."

"I don't remember that," Alice cracked a smile and winked at Samuel, who chuckled at her joke.

"Come on, mom." Tom laughed. "A dementia joke? Really? You know better. Have you heard from Jay?"

"No," Alice tore into her sandwich again and spoke through a mouthful of ham. "He doesn't call as often as he should. Haven't heard from Harmony, either."

*Harmony's gone, mom,* thought Tom, but he dared not say it. "Jason's busy, mom. We're all flying up there for mother's day though. It'll only be a few months."

"I'm looking forward to it," Alice smiled. "Nobody visits me anymore, except for Samuel."

"I do what I can," Samuel said. "Someone's gotta make sure she eats her sandwiches."

Tom smiled, pulling his phone away from his ear long enough to check the time and for notifications. "Listen, mom," he said, "when we come down for mother's day, we want to drive back out to the homestead, visit the old stomping grounds. Do you want to come with?"

"Anything to get out of here," sighed Alice. "I hate periwinkle."

"Sure, we can drive out there Sunday afternoon and visit dad and Harm." Tom was unable to stop himself, and swore silently.

In Alaska, Alice's face perked up. "Harmony's there? She hasn't called me."

"Yeah, mom," sighed Tom. "Harm's there."

"Please, Tom, tell her and Jason both to call me."

"Will do," Tom said. "Isa and the girls say hi."

"Oh, I love them," Alice smiled. "How old are they now?"

"Oh, they're getting so big you wouldn't believe it. Nat's seven and can ride a bike now, and Emma's five and reading."

Alice's smile stretched wider, becoming an ear-to-ear grin. "Will you bring them to Anchorage in May then?"

"Yes, mom."

"Promise?"

"I promise."

---

Deputy Davis was a strange, lanky man who spoke a little too slow. His face was a blur of unwashed short curly auburn beard hairs, and he smelled of menthol cigarettes. When he talked in that slow pace of his, he lingered for too long on the "s" and "t" sounds. Tom thought it made him sound like a lizard person. He had Tom lead him into Harmony's Queendom, following along the driveway leading up to the double-track dirt road, then hooking right along the barbed wire fence that delineated the property line. From here, they struck out east across a deer path littered with disturbed pine needles, sticks plunged into the ground, and other signs of play to Harmony's Castle, a fortress secluded in a tight grove of pine trees made of sticks and branches bound together with twine and camouflaged under the pine needles.

"This is Harm's castle," Tom said. "This is where she'd be."

"Harmony?" Davis called. "Harmony, are you t-there? Your family is-s looking for you!"

Deputy Davis' voice echoed into the woods, but no response came. Tom approached the castle for himself, peeking inside. "She's not there," he shook his head.

"Where els-se might-t s-she be?" Davis asked.

Tom shrugged. "It's a big queendom. We own about a hundred acres. Follow me."

Tom and Deputy Davis trekked further from the driveway into the forest, Tom acting as the guide and giving Davis the tour of the Queendom. He pointed out the location of battles they had, of monuments and landmarks, and the little magical bits that added depth and lore to their imaginative wonderland. Jason in particular was a big connoisseur of fantasy, and he had instilled a love of his genre of choice upon his younger siblings. Thus, they had spent countless days in these woods playing Kingdoms, and whether or not there had originally been magic here a decade ago when the Carlini family bought the acreage, the Carlini siblings had filled the forest to the brim with wonder and mystery. Now, Tom's intensive knowledge of the woods paid off as he was able to help Davis search every nook and cranny for Harmony.

As they searched, Deputy Davis said, "Don't-t worry, kids-s get-t los-st-t in t-the woods-s all t-the t-time. We'll find her." He repeated this several times, which started to stir up a certain degree of uneasiness in Tom. Despite his mother's wailing and fear, Tom was already confident that Harmony was alright, but the repeated reassurances from the sheriff's deputy started to concern him that Harmony might actually be in some real danger after all. Still, even though it felt like a vast and wild expanse to an eleven year old, Harm's Queendom wasn't much bigger than a few acres, and they were able to search it in fairly reasonable time, though they found no sign of Harmony Carlini.

Across the property, Jason and Sheriff Callahan struck out towards the South. Jason took a much more practical approach to looking for Harmony, but as he was traveling through his own Kingdom he was much more familiar with that particular stretch of forest. He and Sheriff Callahan checked his own castle and throne-room, which Harmony was never allowed to enter, but of course she wasn't there. They made their way down to the gully towards the southern end of the property that marked the border between Jason's Kingdom and Tom's Kingdom. Here, Callahan walked up and down the mile-long length of the gully, which varied from a few feet to several yards deep and wide, calling for Harmony. Once they ruled out the gully, they headed south to the swimming hole.

The swimming hole had originally been a quarry, where crushed rock and gravel had been dug out to construct the Carlini's driveway. Similar quarries dotted the Alaskan landscape, but this one was created by the Carlinis for the Carlinis. The kids called it Lake Trinity, in honor of the shared history of their three kingdoms. On hot summer afternoons where the atmosphere was thin, the sun never set, and the air lapped up every bit of moisture it could find, a truce would be called between the Kingdoms and the Carlini kids would trek down to the swimming hole, accessed by an ill-maintained dirt roadway overgrown with wispy grass and weeds, and cool off all afternoon long. It had always been a safe and happy place, and Jason hoped now that if something had driven Harmony off of the homestead, she would have gone to Lake Trinity to wait it out.

---

Andrew Callahan sat up and wiped vomit off his chin. He had been sitting, almost lying, next to the corpse of the monstrous bear and the scattered remains of his partner for who-knows-how-long. Dingo had fallen asleep next to his master, seemingly not understanding death. He would need to call for backup. He would need the coroner, or someone, to come out and deal with the mess that had been Nathan Carlini. He would need medical attention himself - he was bleeding from multiple cuts and scrapes, some of which the bear had caused, some not, and he was pretty sure he had a broken rib. Most importantly, he would need a drink.

"Fuck," he muttered under his breath, then repeated the word until it escalated like an avalanche, first almost a whisper, then a stern reprimand, then a shout, and finally a wail. "Fuck, fuck, fuck, fuck, FUCK!" He held back hot tears, a mixture of anger and anguish, and instead released a primal yell. Dingo cowered, but did not retreat. He was a good dog.

Callahan held out his hand for the dog, and it came to him reluctantly. "Good dog," he muttered, trying to sound reassuring but wildly failing. Callahan tried not to look at Nathan's remains but caught himself staring. He simply didn't have a head anymore, but he imagined him staring back at him. *Poor Alice,* he thought. *Poor boys. Would Nathan at least be reunited with his daughter in death?* He certainly hoped so.

"I'm sorry, Nathan," he finally sobbed to the corpse. "I'm sorry. I'm sorry. I failed you. I could've saved you."

The dog whined and sat next to him, looking at him with its big eyes as if to say, *bring him back.* Callahan petted the dog and heaved between sobs.

"I can't bring him back," he said, "I can't bring Harmony back either, but I can protect the others. I will protect the others. I'll take care of them real good. For you, Nathan. I promise. I swear."

## Chapter Five

"I talked to mom the other day," Tom said, "on the phone."

On Tom's laptop screen, Doctor Meyer cocked her head slightly and pursed her lips. "Oh yeah?" she asked. "How is she?"

"She's doing good," Tom answered, "all things considered. She's excited for the Mother's Day trip. I know we really shouldn't be traveling during a pandemic, but neither of us have seen her in almost a year. Hell, I haven't seen Jace in almost a year."

"There's something you're not telling me, isn't there?"

Tom sighed. "She thinks Harmony's coming."

Doctor Meyer chewed her thoughts for a minute, the way Tom had gotten accustomed to her doing. "I see…" she wrote something down in her notepad. "And what about your dad?"

"She said she missed him," answered Tom. "I suppose that's something. She both remembered him and remembered that he's not with us anymore."

"That's good for her," smiled Doctor Meyer, but her face fell when Tom remained serious.

"I'm not so sure it is," he sighed. "Her doctor, Samuel, told me that patients get better for a week or so right before they…" Tom's words trailed off. He couldn't vocalize the thought of losing his mother. Doctor Meyer remained silent for a minute or two, before Tom spoke again. "It's a good thing we're already planning on going up there next week."

"I'm sure she'll be fine," Doctor Meyer tried to reassure Tom, but she didn't even quite believe her own words. She thought for a second, then added something she knew was true. "Your mother loves her boys very much."

---

Jason and Sheriff Callahan had searched the entire trail down to the swimming hole and back up, following the ravine as far as they could before cutting back towards the house, and had found no sign of Harmony Carlini. When they made it back to the house, Alice was waiting on the porch with sandwiches.

"Did you find her?" Alice asked, already knowing the answer.

Sheriff Callahan had taken his hat off and held it to his chest. “No, ma’am. No sign of her.”

Alice frowned. “I, uh, I searched the house inside and out, plus the whole yard, garage, chicken coop, and everything. Called my husband, too. Thought he might have her, but he said she came out to watch him drive down the driveway and he hasn’t seen her since. He said he’s heading back just as soon as he can.” She held up the platter. “Figured you boys would be hungry, so I made sandwiches.”

“Thank you,” Sheriff Callahan said as he took a sandwich off the plate. “I’m going to my car to call for backup. If she’s not on the property, she’s somewhere nearby. Maybe even get a chopper in the air, get dogs out here, whatever it takes to find her.” He perched his hat back atop his head and set off at a brisk pace around the house to where his cruiser was parked.

Alice turned her attention to Tom. “Are you okay, Thomas?”

Tom shrugged. “I’m worried, I suppose. It’s not like Harmony to run off.”

Alice handed Tom a sandwich. “I know. We’ll find her. Don’t worry. Your dad’s on his way back up here, too.” She paused for a second in thought, trying her hardest to believe the words she was saying. “Harmony knows these woods like the back of her hand, you know. I guarantee you she’s not actually lost, just adventuring.”

“I know,” Tom said. It was a lie though. Each time someone assured him that his sister was okay, it made him believe it a little less.

---

Every time Tom came back to Alaska, it blew him away how big the state was. Sure, the midwest had a lot of space, but Alaska was on an entirely different level. After getting off his plane in Anchorage and into their metallic green rental economy hatchback, which took an hour in and of itself, he still had a five hour drive out to the estate. Jason had flown out the night before, picked up mom from her apartment, and driven out to the property in time to eat dinner there and spend the night in his old bedroom, so they were just waiting on the Midwest Carlinis.

The weekend was sure to be a somber function. It seemed that nothing brought the Carlini family together like a funeral, and sure enough Tom had heard that relatives he hadn't even thought about in years had come out of the woodwork to come see his father goodbye. *It makes sense,* he thought. *Nathan Carlini was a good man. Well loved by many.* In fact, if Nathan had his way, his funeral would've probably been televised with a crowd of thousands in attendance, but the memorial service wasn't really about Nathan as much as it was for Alice. Funerals, after all, are for the living.

Still, it was a beautiful day, and traffic was light on the drive. Tom was able to turn on cruise control and enjoy himself, while Isabel reclined in the passenger seat, her eyes mostly closed and her headphones on, with her book-on-tape playing softly over the drone of tires on asphalt. Tom was alone with the road and his thoughts.

The last time Tom had seen his dad was about a year prior. He had a work thing, some kind of convention for government workers, in Saint Louis, and had used Tom's guest bedroom in Kansas City as a free hotel room for the night. He'd shown up at about eight-thirty, they had bonded over a beer and some television - Nathan eating two slices of leftover pizza since he hadn't had dinner yet - and Tom had gone upstairs to finish some work leaving Nathan to sleep on the couch. When he woke up in the morning, his father had left early to beat the I-70 traffic through downtown. He hadn't even seen Isabel on that trip since she had started working evenings to help pay for their wedding. Hell, he never actually got to see Isabel since they had gotten engaged, much less married. He'd been out in the field on their wedding day and had missed it altogether.

Tom's relationship with his father, after all, had been complicated. Sure, he had loved his dad. All three of the Carlini children had. Dad getting home from work was always an event, and they loved those mornings when they were awake to chase him down the driveway as he left. When he got to spend an extra week at home, they would often go out into the woods together and Nathan would listen to the birds and quiz the children on which species sang which song. After the children had established their kingdoms, it was Nathan who helped them build fortresses and battlements in the woods. He had been an Eagle Scout when he was younger, and was eager to teach his offspring every knot and lashing that he knew.

That wasn't the only side to Nathan Carlini though. He was occasionally a volatile man, easily angered and quick to lash out. More than once, he had yelled at Tom for something that shouldn't have been a big deal, and on a few occasions he had actually struck him. "It's the way he was raised," Tom's mother would explain. "Spare the rod and spoil the child, all that Christian stuff. He's a product of a different time." These were kind words, but they never actually did much to soothe the stinging sensation on Tom's freshly paddled ass. His mother could insist that his father still loved him all that she wanted, but he had seen his father's face when he lashed out and struck him. That kind of thing leaves a mark, not just the red one across Tom's buttocks, but one that lasted with him into the twenty-first century.

After Harmony disappeared, he got worse, too. Nathan didn't go into the woods anymore. He never fished with the boys or went on hiking trips, though the boys also grew disenfranchised with the mountains' offerings after the loss of their sister. Still, Nathan seemed to be gone for longer and longer stretches every time, and when he was home he was often either on his phone and computer in the master bedroom talking with who-knows-who into the odd hours of the night or lounging out in a nearly vegetative state in front of the television in the living room, his shirt flung haphazardly over the back of the couch and a beer in his hand, breath reeking of stale cigarettes which he never seemed to have the time to smoke before the loss of his daughter. This was the Nathan Carlini that Tom had left behind when he moved to Kansas City for school, and this was much closer to the Nathan Carlini that spent eight hours on Tom's couch in 2001. Tom hated to say it, but this was the Nathan Carlini who was killed in a tragic hunting accident, and who they were traveling to bury in the Alaskan Mountains he once loved so very dearly.

Tom had made this drive hundreds of times before, and he auto-piloted off the Pioneer exit ramp without letting it break his chain of thought. The green hatchback left the four-lane highway and entered the countryside without so much as disturbing Isabel from her audiobook. *It's a shame,* thought

Tom. *She's not even taking in the countryside. Her eyes are closed.* Tom had seen these mountains a hundred times before, but as they left the city behind them and drove further into the wilderness he couldn't help but feel a boy-like sense of wonder at the sheer size of the mountains, all scaled in emerald trees with their peaks disappearing into the low, hazy, grey ether above them. A few miles later, they made a right in the tiny town of Talkeetna. Tom tapped Isabel on the shoulder and she took off her headphones for long enough for him to say, "That's my high school right there."

Isabel nodded and re-donned her headphones, saying "I'm almost done with this chapter, babe. Five more minutes."

*Whatever,* Tom thought. *Five more minutes and we'll be there.*

Another thought entered Tom's mind. It was going to be weird, wasn't it? All seeing each other again? Him, Jason, and Mom all together in the same room for the first time in, what, at least three years or so? And to have it be on the property a mere hundred yards from Harmony's grave - certainly the weekend was not going to be easy.

Twenty more minutes passed. The two-lane road with its yellow double-ribbon dividing Tom's car from the oncoming traffic fed into an undivided forest lane as the oncoming traffic grew thinner. The curbs dropped away and the shoulders became soft and narrow, and more and more minutes passed between each car that Tom saw. Isabel took off her headphones and commented on how many trees there were, and Tom chuckled to himself. *She can't see the forest though,* he thought. Isabel really was a city girl through and through, despite her midwest upbringing.

Another turn and the asphalt gave way to gravel crunching under the car's tires. Ten more minutes and the gravel disappeared too, fading into hardened grey earth that thudded under the car clumsily, beaten into the shape of a double-track road only by the vehicles - mostly logging trucks and four-wheelers - that had come between the end of the Muddy Season a few weeks prior and now. Tom cranked down his window and breathed in the fresh air, and the two rode in silence, enjoying the sounds of the forest broken only by their own tire noise.

Finally, they made one last right turn past a faded old mailbox that bore the name "CARLINI". The driveway, made of crushed rock over a decade ago, was actually an improvement over the washed out logging road, and Isabel let slip a sigh of relief. They crept up the driveway at a snail's pace - Nathan had taught Tom better than to speed up an unpaved driveway he didn't intend to re-plow - until the house came into view ahead of them, a cluster of cars tightly parked in the front lawn. A black Cadillac hearse was pulled up alongside the front porch, and in it Tom knew lay his father.

## Chapter Six

The woods were logged thin and devoid of nearly anything in 1964, save for a lone double-track logging road which bisected it from the northwest to the southeast. They were nearly untraveled as well, going days or even weeks at a time without seeing so much as a hiker or lone traveler. On one September night, that silence was broken by the sound of a Dodge Power Wagon, which had seen service in World War II but was now utilized for scouting logging locations, coming up the road.

The man driving the Power Wagon had also seen service in World War II. His name was James Elmer "Jimbo" Jonas, and he had landed at Normandy Beach on D-Day to kick some nazi ass. It was while deployed in France that he met a British-Indian soldier named Sanjeet who had introduced him to the concept of Buddhism. He hadn't entirely understood the millennia-old practice, but had liked the nonviolent part of the dogma enough, and inspired by that Gandhi fellow what who starved himself to beat the British he had decided to dedicate himself to a life of nonviolence. So, he went to his commanding officers and requested to go home.

They had laughed at him. “What for,” they asked.

So, he explained as best as he could what Sanjeet had told him about nonviolence and karma and how Gandhi beat the British by not eating until they decided to do the right thing.

And his commanding officers laughed at him again. So he took it up the chain of command, and went to the Captain of his division. He told him about doing unto others and how he wanted to help people, really help people, and not just pump some krauts full of lead and whatnot. So they reassigned him to drive a truck. Instead of shooting the Germans himself, he would be toting ammunition from the landing point in Normandy where they had it shipped in from England and America to the front lines, where it would be given to other soldiers who were more willing to shoot it at the Germans.

Anything you can do to help the war effort.

Anyways, the truck that Jimbo Jonas had driven in France was a Dodge WC military truck, essentially a box van built onto the back of a heavy duty farm truck of the type Dodge had made for half a century. It was a big brute of a vehicle, with bulletproof tires, four-wheel-drive, and a massive no-frills six cylinder engine that made a whole lot of noise and honestly not much power. He remembered the serial number for it due to a pneumonic device he had invented when bored between ammunition runs: "Whiskey-Charlie-one-zero-zero-zero-two-seven-four-four, Gen'ral Ike's mom is a massive whore". Jimbo Jonas had never met General Eisenhower. He had definitely never met the man's mother. Still, the rhyme was easy to remember and it made him chuckle.

After the war, Jimbo returned to his hometown of Chattanooga, Tennessee. He married his high school sweetheart, Irene, and got a job driving a truck up and down the east coast. Of course, then General Eisenhower got elected president and decided to build a highway system to rival the Germans' coast-to-coast, and the trucking industry exploded overnight and became much harder to maintain small businesses in. The company that Jimbo drove trucks for closed in 1960.

Like his own parents thirty years prior, Jimbo found himself out of work, out of money, and out of luck. He and Irene had a kid on the way, so he decided to do what his dad hadn't done thirty years ago and always said he regretted it, and moved out west in search of work. The Jonases moved to Anchorage, where Jimbo searched advertisements for potential jobs until he found one that was a perfect fit: the Skitooa Lumber Milling Company was looking for drivers to drive equipment up to a prospective new lumber-mill site in the Alaskan forest.

Jimbo went in for a job interview the next day, and told them that he had driven WCs in France during the war. They hired him right away, and took him out to the lot to show him his truck. It was a surplus WC from the war, modified lightly to feature an open bed appropriate for carrying heavy equipment up a mountain, and painted with a fresh bright red paint job, under which Jimbo could still make out the old Army serial number:

Whiskey-Charlie-one-zero-zero-zero-two-seven-four-four.

So, Jimbo stuck with the job for some time. Reunited with his truck, he drove up and down those mountain roads for years without incident. Even though the other drivers would carry hunting rifles across the back of the bench seat for protection from bears and moose and whatnot, Jimbo still stuck to his pacifistic ways taught to him by his friend Sanjeet and didn't carry jack shit with him for self defense. And it worked for him for years...

Until September of 1964.

The truck rumbled down the double-track road, the ancient iron motor working overtime to haul its payload up the mountain. Inside, Jimbo Jonas hummed a show-tune to himself, the burnt-out butt of a cigarette still hanging from his lips. He tapped lightly on the steering wheel with his fingertips to keep time, occasionally muttering a phrase or two of lyrics. His eyes were on the road ahead of him, but his mind was on broadway.

There was a blur ahead of him as something big crossed the road. Jimbo stamped the brakes, and the truck's front wheels locked. The back wheels conserved their momentum, weighed down by the equipment on the flatbed behind him, and the truck began to swing sideways, jolting over the ruts left by a thousand uneventful runs up this mountain before. Jimbo pressed the brakes harder, throwing his weight against the steering wheel to countersteer against the skid, and his rear tires seized, now stuck in the rut. The truck slid forward for another dozen yards or so before it hit a muddy patch and released from the rut, snapping sharply to the left. Before Jimbo had time to react, the truck tipped over and he was thrown against the driver side door as it slammed to the ground with a hideous noise.

Now starved of both fuel and oil, the motor seized and sputtered to a stop. Jimbo had hit his head pretty hard on the door, and it took him a minute to process what had just happened. His head hurt, his shoulder hurt, his back hurt. Really, he was in more pain than he had experienced since he had been shot in France in '43. He could feel his warm blood soaking his scalp and dripping down the side of his face. Still, he couldn't break his concentration from the eerie silence of the forest.

Jimbo picked himself up off the truck's door, taking a second to survey the pain radiating from his right shoulder.

He was pretty sure he had broken a bone, but didn't know the extent of the damage yet beyond that. He inhaled deeply, smelling for spilled diesel, but didn't smell anything but the damp smell of the woods, and a putrid scent like a skunk. Did they have skunks in Alaska? He couldn't recall. He fumbled around the footwell for his CB radio receiver, then jammed the button down with his thumb and groaned into it.

"Mayday, mayday, this is Jimbo Jonas with Skitooa Lumber. I've had an accident. I'm injured. My current position is…"

He froze. Something was moving outside the truck. Listening carefully, he could hear the thump-thump of footsteps approaching him. Then, the thing that had crossed the roadway in front of him stepped back into view through the windshield. It was big, taller than any man Jimbo had ever seen, though it walked on two legs like a man. It was covered in tangled orangish-brown hair from head to toe that somewhat shrouded the shape of its body. Its face and upper chest were hairless, deep black skin juxtaposed dramatically against the golden-red hair that covered the rest of the thing.

Beady black eyes, deep-set below a heavy brow ridge, watched Jimbo menacingly.

"What the fuck?" Jimbo asked nobody in particular, throwing himself against the door instinctively to try and escape but fighting the entire weight of the truck in the process. The creature eyed him curiously, then reared to its full height and let out a bellowing, howling roar.

"What the fuck what the fuck what the fuck?" Jimbo frantically pressed against the door handle, then turned and began to climb across the truck to open the right-hand, now upwards-facing door. The creature picked up a dislodged tree limb from the ground and held it over its head with both hands. Roaring again, it broke the limb effortlessly in half and threw both halves at the truck. Jimbo screamed in terror.

And the monster charged. The last thing Jimbo remembered was being pulled through the windscreen of his truck and having his limbs yanked in opposite directions.

---

"How are you doing, you son of a bitch?" Jason hadn't even given Tom the opportunity to get out of his car before he was on him, shattering the somber tone that surrounded the house with his infectious big-brother brand of loving, joyful energy. He extended a hand as Tom opened the door to his rental car, and lifted his little brother out of the vehicle and into a waiting bear hug. "It's been too long, brother. Oh, and what's this?" He nodded at Isabel. "I see you haven't scared her off yet."

"Yeah, and where's your girlfriend?" Tom asked. Isabel smiled and waved timidly at Jason, who was a lot for her to take on a good day.

"She's inside," Jason said. He gently set Tom down and walked around the car, where he gingerly hugged Isabel. "How are you, Isabel?"

"I'm holding on, Jason," she said. "Trying to be here for Tom. I have to admit I didn't know Nathaniel all that well."

"And not for a lack of trying, either," Tom interjected. "The one time the man's visited us since Isa's lived with me, he showed up after she'd gone to bed, crashed on the couch, and was gone by breakfast."

"Yeah," Jason sighed, "that sounds like dad. Always someplace to be, right? Come on, let's go get you all checked in with mom."

Inside the house, the lights were dimmed down low and people milled about, looking at the photographs on the walls and Tom and Jason's old belongings like it was some kind of museum. Elise appeared out of the crowd, her short blonde hair standing in stark contrast to the burgundy dress she wore, and greeted Tom and Isabel, before pointing them in the direction of their mother.

Alice sat at the head of the dining room table, a glass of merlot in one hand and a sober expression on her face as an endless stream of relatives gave her small, half-hearted embraces and offered their condolences. When Jason and Tom entered the room, her face lit up.

"My boys," she said affectionately. "You made good time from Anchorage." Alice rose gingerly to greet her sons.

Tom smiled warmly and eased himself past the chairs around the table to embrace his mother. "Hello, mom. It's been too long. You remember my wife, Isabel?"

"Of course," Alice said as she did a little curtsy. "And you, Jason, you've brought…" She paused, blanking on her name.

"Elise," Jason's girlfriend said, bending to offer her hand to Alice, who smiled with recognition and took it.

"Elise," Alice repeated her name, committing it to memory. "I'm sorry, I've had a rough few weeks."

"It's understandable, mom," Jason reassured her. "Where's dad? I want to go pay my respects."

Alice pointed back into the living room. "The urn is over there, by the television. You best make your rounds, too. Lots of aunts and uncles here that haven't seen you since you were little. Probably don't even recognize you, all grown up." Alice rose out of her chair and finished her drink. "If you'll excuse me, we'll have to catch up later. I need a cigarette to wash down this merlot with."

The four turned and wandered into the living room, issuing polite greetings to relatives as they went. Across the room, they found Nathan's ashes in an elegant urn fashioned from brushed stainless steel, burnished to give it a blackish color. Tom led the others up to the urn, where he sat in silence for a moment. There were many things he wished he could tell his father, after two decades of their complicated relationship, but none of them seemed appropriate to say out loud in a room full of relatives that might as well be strangers. A tear rolled down Tom's cheek, and Isabel wrapped herself around him to comfort him.

"What are they going to do with the ashes," asked Elise.

"There's a plot for him," said Jason, "out front. Off the driveway a little ways, surrounded by some of the oldest trees on the property. It's where we put Harmony's grave, after… you know."

"And mom'll be buried there someday too," Tom muttered. "And you, and me. Here forever on the family property, our little slice of paradise."

Isabel rubbed Tom's back. "Do you want to take her to see it?"

---

A helicopter roared overhead, borrowed from the Alaska State Troopers to aid in the search for Harmony. From its vantage point hundreds of feet in the air, it swept over every square inch of the Carlini property. On the ground, members of the Mat-Su Sheriff Department, led by Sheriff Callahan, were joined by not just state troopers but the entire volunteer fire department as well. Over the past forty-eight hours, news of a little girl's disappearance had spread, and volunteers were beginning to trickle in from the surrounding towns; Talkeetna, Susitna, Trapper Creek, even as far south as Anchorage.

Not everyone who made their way up the treacherous doubletrack road did so in noble search of a missing little girl, however. Word had spread to the press, and the big white vans with letters and numbers emblazoned on their sides with words like "ACTION NEWS" and "WORKING FOR YOU" had arrived, crowding volunteers' cars out of the makeshift parking lot in the clearing around the Carlini property and pointing their antennae towards the sky while opportunistic cameramen swarmed the Carlini house like fishermen angling for a shot of the grieving mother they could show a million viewers at six.

Inside, Alice Carlini had drawn the blinds and was hiding out of sight, trying to carry on normal day-to-day life with the boys while their father, who had rushed home from work as soon as he got the phone call from Sheriff Callahan, searched every nook and cranny of the woods with several dozen volunteers. Presently, the press got too close, and Sheriff Callahan's men were forced to set up a perimeter around the house and beat the press back to the driveway. The story spread far and wide, and every television across the country was telling the story of the little girl lost in the Alaskan wilderness.

The search continued for days. The number of volunteers searching the forest swelled to over a hundred, with helicopters buzzing overhead. Then, the volunteers started giving up one by one, heading back to Talkeetna and Willow to return to their lives. The predatory news crews got scoops in other towns, and hurried off with their giant antenna and their grubby cameramen. The helicopters stopped buzzing overhead, and the Sheriff's Department and State Troopers had to reassign their men to more pressing matters. After about a week, the search was all but given up. Harmony Carlini was never found.

---

The next time Tom and Isabel flew into Alaska in May of 2020, just scheduling a flight was a pain. The world was locked in chaos in the midst of the Coronavirus pandemic, and though the airports were empty, planes had been grounded and flights canceled. They had to take a series of connecting flights to Sacramento, Seattle, and Juneau to be able to make their way up into the interior of the state, before embarking on the three hour drive up into the wilderness towards Skitooa.

Jason had flown out the night before, just like he had promised, and had picked up their mother at her nursing home. With the way her condition was deteriorating, her personal physician Samuel had elected to tag along to ensure her safety, as well as Jason's wife and child. In all, it would be the nine of them on the old property for a mother's day weekend worth remembering. It could, of course, be their last with Alice Carlini, so it was worth making the most out of even with everything that was going on.

The drive into the Alaskan Mountains was still every bit as beautiful as it had been nearly twenty years prior, but the hellions in Tom's backseat made it slightly more difficult to enjoy the trip. Isabel's ears remained unplugged, her current book on tape relegated to the little bits of free time that she got when Tom was working and the girls, who were home from school for who knows how long, were off doing something quiet. The tire noise of the econobox's hard rubber on Alaska's equally hard asphalt was drowned out by screams of delight, the kind made by a ten year old and a six year old who had been instructed to keep themselves busy for six hours.

By the time the Midwest Carlinis had made it up into the mountains, past Talkeetna, and two rights into the woods, the girls were asleep. Tom had his quiet and Isabel was even able to get a few chapters of her audiobook in. Tom's slew of thoughts and emotions were more than enough to keep him occupied as the road turned to the muddy doubletrack through the forest. He largely had pleasant memories of this place still, but every time his eyes were taken off the road ahead of him illuminated by his headlights, he thought he'd catch glimpses of shadows of monsters in the woods. These woods had given him so much, but they had taken even more.

It was about halfway between the last paved road and the driveway to the property that one of these shadows first became a problem. The girls, roused from their slumber by the sudden change in road texture and the bumpy descent into the valley, had begun sleepily bickering with each other. Isabel, on the other hand, had drifted to sleep in the serenity of her audiobook. Tom tried to wait for the girls to figure it out, but to no avail.

"Daaaaad," Emma wailed from the backseat, "tell Natalie to leave me aloooone!"

"Honey?" Tom asked Isabel, "you want to take this one?" Isabel waved her hand dismissively, not wanting to wake up. Tom looked at the girls in the rear view mirror. "Girls, we're almost there. Can you keep it together for just five more minutes?"

"I'm tired!" Natalie mouthed off.

Emma sneered at her sister. "That's because you keep *touching me!*"

"I'm not touching you!" Natalie responded, her finger floating mere inches from her sister's face.

"Natalie, please," Tom pleaded.

Emma reached out and grabbed Natalie's hand, jamming her finger into her own eye socket. "Ow!" she exclaimed. "You are too touching me!"

Tom turned around in his seat, "Girls! That's enough!" He snapped.

"Tom, look out!" Isabel shouted, suddenly roused from her sleep.

Both girls screamed as the car came to a sudden halt. Twisted in his seat, Tom was thrown against the steering wheel. His head came to a rest mere inches from the windshield, which was spider-webbed itself against a mass of tangled orange hair on the outside. Tom slowly looked up to see the mangled shape of some massive animal resting on top of the car, though he couldn't make out any details through the shattered windshield.

"Tom? What was that?" Isabel asked, one of her headphones dangling from her ear.

Tom looked at her slowly, scared to make too sudden a move. "I think it's a bear," he whispered. "Stay very quiet, girls."

"Is it moving?" Emma whimpered. "Is it alive?" Natalie just quietly whimpered to herself.

Tom slowly leaned himself back into his seat, wincing in pain as he turned his body. The airbags hadn't deployed, and his ribs had hit the steering wheel hard. They were definitely bruised, possibly broken. "I don't know," he said. He looked his family up and down. "Is everybody alright?"

Isabel grabbed his arm tightly. "Tom, look!" she hissed.

The glass in the windshield creaked and popped as the furry mass started moving, sliding itself down towards the front of the car. The Carlinis all held their breath, and Tom suddenly wished that he had brought a firearm in his checked luggage. The creature grunted, a chilling sound that Tom didn't quite think sounded entirely natural, but entirely too familiar, too human for his liking. It slid off the car, letting the car lift up freed from its massive weight and knocking out a headlight in the process. Illuminated now only by the moonlight above, it took on a hunched over form and slowly and jerkily hobbled off into the woods on two feet.

Tom let out a sigh of relief as both girls started quietly sobbing in the backseat. He turned to Isabel, who had a look of terror on her face as she mouthed the words, "was that…?" Tom was just glad that the car was still running. Without saying a word, he turned on the brights to get what light he could from the one remaining broken headlamp, and quickly and quietly drove away from the collision site.

## Chapter Seven

Months had passed since Harmony's disappearance, and the Carlini boys had lost interest in the woods. The summer had come and gone with barely a trip to the swimming hole, and their Kingdoms lay dormant beyond the clearing of the house, as untouched by human visitors as they had been twenty thousand years ago before the continent had first been seen by mankind. Instead, the boys elected to sit inside in the air conditioning and safety of the home, watching their favorite cartoon videotapes and playing board games with each other. Though she wouldn't admit it, Alice was a little relieved to not have the boys in the woods. They were, after all, a dangerous place, and the Carlini family wouldn't be able to sustain multiple losses in one year.

It was a crisp Saturday morning in the autumn of 1992. As the days draw short and the northern half of the world descends into winter, the Alaskan Mountains begin to see their first frost and even snow in the waning daylight hours. It was on one such morning, with a fresh dusting of loose powder draped across the mountains, that Tom Carlini decided that he was ready to reclaim his forest.

A few months prior, back in September, his father had purchased for him a Daisy 880 Red Rider air rifle, definitely a treasure for a ten year old boy. He had been out in the yard several times since then, where Jason had taught him how to shoot it at his targets of choice, be they tin cans or squirrels. Armed with their air rifle, the boys had slowly started adventuring further and further out into their woods, though they still hadn't managed to get further than eyesight from the house. They were convinced that something had taken Harmony, like Sheriff Callahan had said, and that if they ventured too far they would be taken too. It's no way to live, though, in fear of what you love, and they had hatched a plan together to band up during their fall break and reclaim their Kingdoms.

The plan was simple enough. The boys would set out across Tomland, which they still considered friendly territory, headed north along the driveway to the property fence at the doubletrack dirt road. Here, they would set out east and into Harmony's Queendom, following the fenceline a mere three to ten yards from the road, so that if going got too tough they would be able to make their way out to terrain that was easier to traverse. They would cut through Harm's Queendom to the fenceline on the eastern boundary of the property, then set off to the south until they once again made the friendly territory of Jason's Kingdom bordered to the north by the ravine, which they would then follow down to the dirt road that led to the old hunting cabin and the quarry-slash-swimming-hole. They would then follow that dirt road back. Though it felt like they were going to war, the mission was really more exploratory than anything. Nobody had stepped foot in the Queendom for months, since they buried Harmony's favorite dress in a little casket by the driveway on the north side of the property, so their quest was less to actually reclaim the property from whatever fate had befallen their sister and more reclaim it from the air of mystery and danger that had beset it ever since.

The Carlini boys were no strangers to waking up early on Saturdays, but on that Saturday morning they were up particularly early, well before the autumn sun peeked over the mountains to the east. They suited up in their boots and jackets, took Tom's Daisy air rifle and the plaster-of-paris in case they found cool tracks, turned on cartoons in the living room so it seemed like a normal Saturday morning to anyone who was just listening, and set out north down the driveway.

The sun filtered through the thinly needled spruce branches, illuminating the forest floor with the golden light of dawn diffused by a dense autumnal fog, and scattering sparkles everywhere through the thin layer of snow, reminding Tom and Jason of Narnia as they traveled and only serving to amplify the magic that they hoped to reclaim in their kingdoms. Chickadees flitted about in the trees on either side of the driveway, peeping busily to themselves as they scavenged for pine-nuts. The sound of the birds and the crunch of snow and gravel under the boys' boots seemed like the only sounds in the world, and the valley lay otherwise silent sprawling out for miles in any direction from them. It relieved the boys greatly that, even on the border of the Queendom, the magic that they had loved in the woods was still all around them.

The boys reached the fenceline near the doubletrack logging road, where they could no longer see the house around the slight bend in the driveway. Almost a mile back the way they came was the house, warm and safe, with smoke pouring out of the chimney and hot breakfast to be served in a few mere hours. Another ten yards or so to the north was the doubletrack logging road, on the side of which sat the mailbox that Sheriff Callahan's wife, Shannon, had specially painted with the name "CARLINI", as a homemaking gift for the grieving family. Their excursion into the woods now felt more real, as they couldn't even call for help anymore if they needed it. Striking out to the east from the driveway along the fenceline was a trail just wide enough for the two of them to walk side by side. This trail had been blazed by their father earlier that summer, and they both knew it led to Harmony's grave. It didn't matter. The grave was empty, they both knew that. Though everyone was certain that Harmony was dead, they had never found a body or anything. Alice had simply demanded a Christian funeral for her daughter, so they had buried a nice pine box with her favorite dress and some of her cherished possessions in it in her place. As they approached the gravesite, it was an odd comfort to remember that it lay empty.

Jason held up his hand to Tom to stop, and the boys paused their march. Stooping to the ground, Jace plucked a small white rain-lily. He solemnly approached the empty grave and knelt before it, gingerly placing the flower next to the wooden cross that marked the girl's ceremonial final resting place. Tom silently bowed his head out of respect for his brother's ritual, and the brothers shared a moment of silence in respect for their sister. This excursion, after all, was dedicated to her.

After a moment, the boys locked eyes. They silently rose to their feet and gathered their things, and continued on their journey. The trail that their father had blazed ended here, but a natural deerpath had formed along the barbed-wire fence that bordered the northern edge of the Carlini property, which they followed to the east. The forest closed in on them to the right, with the barbed wire blocking their egress to the left, and the woods began to feel hot and claustrophobic despite the layer of snow on the ground.

The chickadees which had been buzzing about happily near the driveway did not follow the boys further into the woods, and their cheep-cheeps grew further and further away, replaced only by deafening silence. Only their own breath and their footsteps crunching in the fresh powdered snow remained, aside from the occasional squirrel rutting around on the forest floor, making a noise like a much larger creature in the murky woods. Tom and Jason marched on, Tom with his Daisy air rifle propped against his shoulder like a soldier off to war.

It wasn't much more than a mile before the boys arrived at the offshoot path towards their next landmark - the North Gate. This was the next crossing across the barbed wire fence where the boys could leave the deer-path behind and take the logging road on the rest of their trip. The road would be an easier path - though it was eroded by disuse and disrepair and only traversable by horse, foot, or four-wheeler, it was wider than the deerpath and provided greater visibility - but technically it wasn't on the Carlini property and Tom wasn't sure it would really count as reclaiming Harm's Queendom. He was mulling over whether or not he wanted to ask his brother about moving at the risk of sounding like a chicken when Jason spoke up.

"Tom, do you think we should take the logging road?"

Tom tried to pretend as if he hadn't just had the exact same thought. "Why'd we do that, Jace?" He asked.

"I was just thinking," Jason replied, "it'd be easier to walk and safer out in the open. We could consider it a shortcut to the eastern fence-line."

"You think she might've gone that way?" Tom asked. "Harmony?"

Jason fell silent. He looked out across the North Gate and mulled over his thoughts for a minute, then shook his head. "I don't know, Tom. 'T'ain't her Queendom though, that's for sure."

Tom sighed. "You're right. We're out here to reclaim our woods. That's not ours or the woods."

"We could at least check it out, though."

"We could. Come on."

The boys continued eastward down the fence-line deer-path until they crested a little bluff. Up ahead, they could see the Northern Gate. The tree, once a majestic pole-pine seventy feet tall, had fallen in a storm years before and taken a portion of the fence out with it. The barbed wire now lay on the ground, intertwined with bramblous undergrowth to where it lay like a trap under the thorns and snow. The only way to cross safely and reach the logging road was the trunk of the pole-pine itself, severed at the logging road some twenty feet away by some adventurous explorer with a four-wheeler and a chainsaw, but still extending over the downed fence and across the deer-path well onto the Carlini Property, bleached white with age almost to the point where it blended into the snow around and on top of it.

Tom led his brother down to the North Gate, eyeing the trail ahead and the logging road and comparing the two possible routes. Suddenly, he froze, almost causing Jason to bump into him from behind.

"What is it, Tom," asked Jason.

"Look," Tom whispered, "there on the log."

The snow on the log was a fine powder similar to everywhere else. It had fallen at about five that morning, a mere three hours or so ago. Since then, the snow everywhere else had been untouched, but across the log lay a set of large tracks which resembled bare human feet, but larger and broader.

"Jason, what is that?" Tom asked.

Jason leaned over the track to get a better look. It wasn't the only track on the ground - the tracks crossed the bridge from the logging road and disappeared into the dense forest of the Carlini Property as if they were following a trail into the undergrowth that didn't actually exist - but it was definitely the most clear. "I don't know, Tom," Jason responded after thinking for a second. "Looks like a damned big bear to me."

Tom held his hand across the track, several inches up so he wouldn't disturb it, and muttered to himself "a damn big something," before turning to his brother. "What should we do? It looks like it came from the logging road and is in the woods now. Should we take the logging road?"

"I don't know, Tom," Jason said, "it could've… it could've been the one to…" He stumbled over his words. "Tom, it could've been the one to take Harmony."

"I'm not afraid of no bear," Tom puffed out his chest and assured his brother.

"No, that's not what I mean. It's going to be fifty degrees today, and sunny too. Tom, the snow's gonna melt and take this track with it. These tracks are evidence."

"Do you think we could use the plaster?" Tom mused.

Jason shook his head. "It's not gonna work well in the snow. Remember the lynx tracks we found last spring? The plaster turned to mush and didn't set right in the cold. No, we're going to need a camera."

---

The little blue rental car hissed angrily as Tom pulled it up the familiar driveway and into the yard of the Carlini family home, where he parked it in the grass next to Jason's pickup truck. He switched the ignition off, then sat back in his seat and sighed. After a minute, he turned to the other Midwest Carlinis, all disheveled and sprawled across their seats in various states of despair. "Everyone alright?" He asked.

"Daddy, what did we hit?" asked his younger daughter.

"Nothing, Natalie," said Isabel.

"It was something," Emma Lee said, "I know it was something, dad, a big something."

"Daddy," Nat asked, "did you hit a monster?"

"No," Tom said, "we didn't hit a monster."

“It was a deer,” Isabel asserted. “Right, Tom? Did we hit a moose?”

“Yeah,” Tom sighed, “a moose.” Somewhere in the back of his mind a memory he had long since buried started to raise its hairy head, but he swallowed it and turned around in his seat. “We’re all okay though, right?” Emma Lee and Natalie nodded and grinned. “Good,” he unbuckled his seatbelt. “Let’s go see Grandma.”

Tom and Isabel climbed out of the car and helped the girls out. Isabel took them up to the house, while Tom stayed behind to survey the damage. Using the flashlight app on his phone, he looked the car up and down. The bumper cover was cracked in two places and hanging on by a single plastic clip. The radiator was hissing as a steady stream of steam shot out through the front grill. The hood was crumpled like tin foil that had been pressed into by a giant thumb, and the windshield was spider-webbed. The one headlight that hadn’t popped out entirely was cracked and slightly cocked, and in the rubber sealant around it...

Tom bent down to get a closer look, plucking out a tuft of coarse reddish-brown hair from the seam. He sniffed it, recoiling suddenly at its pungent, skunk-like odor, as the memories flooded back to him of the parts of his childhood that he had tried to forget. A chill ran up his spine despite the warm summer breeze, and he lifted his phone's flashlight to the trees to scan the forest's edge around him for watching eyes. Slowly, without turning his back to the forest, he popped the "lock" button on the keyfob and took several steps backwards towards the house before turning and hurrying inside.

In the house, Jason and Elise were helping the girls set up their temporary guest suite for the night on the couch. Isabel was sitting on the couch staring off into space, and stood up suddenly when the door closed behind Tom. She crossed the room to him quickly and embraced him, burying her face in his chest. "Tom," she gasped, almost a sob, "is the car okay?"

"Radiator's leaking, but it's nothing Jason and I can't fix," Tom replied. "The rental company's gonna make us pay for it, though."

After a minute, she spoke again in a low voice. "Tom? What did we hit?"

"Something," Tom responded, glancing towards the window. "A damned big something."

## Chapter Eight

Wasilla was about the closest thing you could find to a suburb in Alaska. Nestled outside of Anchorage in the mountainous foothills, the entire town furnished sweeping vistas of perhaps the most beautiful part of the country. Many families, disillusioned with city life but unable or unwilling to dedicate themselves to true wilderness lifestyles, found themselves living in the middle ground of Wasilla.

Due to the high number of families, Wasilla also had a high concentration of teenagers. Many families came from military backgrounds, so many of the teenagers would often seek to escape their strict military parents and slip out into the night for some shenanigans, especially during the perpetual daylight of the Alaskan Summer. It was on one such summer night that two teenage lovers, Dakota and Annie, found themselves "out for a drive" through Wasilla's scenic mountain byways in Dakota's old, beat up Ford Ranger. They found themselves lazily driving down Schwald Road, a popular lovers' lane, on this particular night.

"Why don't we pull over?" asked Dakota. Annie shyly agreed.

The midnight sun was perhaps brighter than Dakota would have liked, but aside from another car parked a few hundred feet ahead they were alone, and that's all that really mattered to the two. Annie undid her seatbelt, and slid across the bench seat to Dakota's waiting arms, where he smiled and gave her a kiss. "Hi, Miss Annie," he grinned coyly.

"Why, Dakota, if I didn't know better, I'd think you were hitting on me," she teased before going in for another kiss. The two paused for a moment, lingering in anticipation, then began a heated makeout session, the same as many that they had enjoyed before.

The car ahead of them started its engine and drove off suddenly and quite quickly. Annie pulled herself off of her boyfriend. "What was that?" She asked shakily.

Dakota scanned the mirrors. No cops. He clumsily suggested, "I don't know. Maybe they're late for a movie?"

Annie thought for a second then shrugged. She leaned in for another kiss as Dakota's hand shakily found its way up the front of her shirt. She reached down and gingerly guided his hand.

*Tok. Tok. Tok.*

A knocking sound rang out through the forest, loud enough to be heard through the truck's closed windows. Dakota paused. "What was that?" He whispered.

"What was what?" Annie asked, slightly disappointed.

"That sound. That knocking sound."

Annie paused and cocked her head as she listened closely, then shook her head. "Dakota, I don't hear anything," she giggled as she leaned in for another kiss.

*Boom!* Something clattered off the roof of the pickup truck, leaving a melon-sized dent poking downwards into the cabin over Annie's head. Both teenagers screamed in shock, heads swiveling to figure out where the sound had come from. A rock about the size of a baseball rolled to a rest in the road near the car, having been thrown from the right. Annie slowly turned her head to the right where the rock had been thrown from and screamed.

Dakota didn't even see the second rock coming before it smashed through the passenger side window of the truck and hit Annie square in the forehead. Hot blood splashed across his windshield, spattering his face and blurring his vision as his girlfriend slumped sideways on top of him. Instinctively, he dropped down alongside her, silently feeling for a pulse. It was weak, but it was there. She was bleeding profusely from the forehead, where the rock had left a contusion so dramatic that he could feel the jagged bone under her skin.

Dakota heard a rustling noise outside, then a snort. He looked up slowly and found himself face to face with a massive ape. Orange shaggy hair framed its face, which was black and bare. As he stared in horror, it stared back at him with empty eyes and its face contorted as its lips peeled back into a large sardonic grin, exposing sharp canine teeth the size of railroad spikes. Its large, grubby hands reached in on either side of the window as it attempted to climb into the truck, not fitting past its massive shoulders. The ridge atop its head rubbed against the roof of the truck, and Dakota felt its hot breath across its face as it fogged the windshield. It struggled to reach him, snapping its jaws inches away from his face, then let out a mighty bellow of frustration that left him deafened momentarily.

Slowly, it withdrew from the vehicle, keeping its weight on the Ranger as it sized up the situation. Moving its massive hand to the hood of the car, it began to round the front of the vehicle. Dakota panicked. He didn't know what else to do. He was totally unarmed and had no way to fight off an animal attack, especially not from an animal of this size. His only hope was trying to scare off the creature. As the ape moved across the front of the truck, he laid on the horn.

The sasquatch was startled by the sound and drew back a step, before roaring and smacking an angry, open palm a foot wide on the hood in anger. Fumbling for his keys, Dakota started the Ford, slammed it in gear, and mashed the accelerator. The truck lurched forward and smacked into the creature, knocking it onto the hood. It rolled off onto the ground and collapsed in the roadway. Dakota didn't look back to see if it stood back up. He didn't stop driving until he reached the hospital. He didn't even stop to think about what the hell he just saw. It was just too terrifying. His focus was on saving Annie anyhow.

---

Alice and Nathaniel were still asleep when Jason returned to the house for the camera. Nathaniel had just gotten back in from work the night before, and Jason knew they'd spend all day in bed together like they always did. Still, he wasn't sure whether they were awake or not. He tiptoed down the hall to their bedroom and opened the door just a crack, sticking his face in and whispering "Mom? Mom?"

Alice Carlini didn't stir. She and Nathan lay motionless in the bed, wrapped around each other. Nathaniel Carlini was snoring. Jason smiled and pushed the door open a little wider and crept inside. He took his mom's polaroid camera off the dresser and tucked it into his coat-pocket.

Turning to leave the room, his eye was caught by the open closet door. Inside the closet, he knew, was his dad's centerfire .308 hunting rifle, which he knew would be a lot more protection against a bear or... whatever than Tom's little air rifle. His dad would flay him alive if he stole it, but it's possible that the monster in the forest would kill him if he didn't. He made the snap-decision that he'd rather face his father even than a monster unarmed.

Jason silently crossed the room and entered the closet, emerging a minute later with the rifle and a box of cartridges. He checked over his shoulder one final time to make sure that his parents were still asleep and quickly and quietly retreated to the living room.

"Did you get the camera?" Tom whispered, before spotting the firearm slung over his brother's shoulder. "Holy shit, Jay, that's dad's gun!"

Jason scowled. "Quiet down or they'll hear you, shit-for-brains!" He hissed.

"Sorry", Tom mouthed the word. He took a second to gather himself, then nodded towards the front door, as if to say "let's go".

Once the Carlini boys were back in the open air away from the house, they were able to talk more freely. Tom looked Jason up and down carrying the rifle slung over his shoulder, a dozen or so cartridges rattling loosely in his coat-pocket. He thought it made his brother look heroic, like a soldier headed to battle an unseen enemy. In comparison, Tom's air rifle - gripped white-knuckled in his hands and held unevenly in front of his body - looked and felt like a toy, but he would still rather have it than nothing today.

This time, the boys backtracked all the way down the driveway to the logging road, and struck out along it eastwards to the North Gate. When they reached the downed tree across the barbed wire, Jason passed Tom the rifle and mounted the log with their mother's camera. He crossed until he could see the footprints - thankfully not yet melted in the waxing sunlight - and snapped a few photographs, which he stuffed in his coat-pocket for protection until they could develop. He then signaled for Tom to come, and Tom crossed the North Gate back into the woods.

Jason handed Tom the camera and told him to snap a few more pictures of the footprints showcasing their size, orientation, and location, using his own foot for reference, then to mix some plaster of paris and take castings. While Tom set about working on the footprints, Jason checked the .308 to ensure that it was loaded and ready to fire. He drew it, pointed at a tree in the distance in the opposite direction of the road or the house, and looked down its scope. Satisfied with the sighting, he then double-checked the safety and slung the rifle back over his shoulder. He turned to his brother. "Got the cast?" He asked.

"The plaster's poured," Tom replied, "but it'll just take a while to completely set."

Jason chewed on his thoughts for a second. "We can come back to it," he decided. "We really ought to keep moving. It's a big set of woods and I want to be back home before dad finds out I borrowed his rifle."

Tom sighed. His brother was right, though. They best be moving. "Alright," he said, "lead the way."

The boys set out eastward again down the trail that ran along the northern fence. After a few minutes of marching in silence, Tom piped up. "Jason?"

"What is it, Tom?"

"You're sure you know how to use that rifle?"

"Yes, Tom," Jason sighed. "Dad taught me when I turned thirteen, remember?"

"That's good," Tom replied. "That's why you're using it then, I suppose. I have no real idea how to use it."

"Plus," Jason said, "I'm closer to being an adult. And bigger, too. This thing would knock you on your scrawny ass."

Tom furrowed his eyebrow deeply. "I know how to use the 880 though," he said, lifting up his Daisy for emphasis. Jason didn't react, so Tom continued. "It's simple.

You just pump the lever a few times, point it, and pull the trigger."

"Uh huh," Jason muttered.

"The more times you pump the lever, the harder it shoots, see? Five pumps'll knock a bird out of the sky. Eight pumps will kill a squirrel or a mouse." Jason didn't respond, so Tom continued. "Dad says you're never supposed to pump it more than ten times, but I figure Bigfoot's real big, huh? How many times do you think we'd have to pump it to kill Bigfoot?"

Jason paused and turned back towards his brother, hazarding a guess. "Eleven?"

Tom chewed on his lip for a second while he did the arithmetic in his head. "I reckon eleven would do it, huh? Ten plus one for good luck. Plus if it doesn't kill him you just follow up and shoot him in the face with dad's rifle, huh?"

Jason turned back forwards and continued walking down the trail in silence for a minute, before Tom piped back up. "That's why you're carrying the real gun. You know how to use that one and I know how to use this one. I don't know about levers and bolts and cartridges, but I can count to eleven pumps. Dad taught you how to use the hunting rifle on your thirteenth birthday. Do you think he'll teach me how to use the hunting rifle on my thirteenth birthday?"

"We'll have to see, Tom. Now quiet down or he'll hear us."

"Oh, okay." Tom piped down and the two vigilantly ventured down the deer-path together into the woods.

---

The children were tired from the long drive anyway, so after a quick round of hugs it wasn't difficult to get them to go to bed. Alice, too, was exhausted from the drive and in a weird mood, probably from being back on the property. She had Jason walk her to Nathan's grave earlier that day, and had been worn out after the physical exercise, so she had gone down for a nap and had not yet awakened. Once they were down, Tom joined Jason and the other adults in the kitchen.

"Beer?" Jason asked. Tom nodded, and Jason tossed him a Pabst.

"Thank you," Tom said, as he cracked the can and took a sip.

"So Tom," Jason asked, smirking. "I saw your rental out there, the little Mitsubishi? It looked pretty FUBAR. What the hell did you hit?"

"Oh, nothing," Isabel said. "It was a moose. Nothing to worry about."

Jason chuckled. "Pretty fuckin' big moose. That's what you get for letting my brother drive." He laughed, and scanned the room, but when his eyes fell on Tom's somber face he quickly clammed up. "Tom?"

"It wasn't a moose, Jace," Tom said. "I think it was... him."

Jason's heart dropped, and his face with it. "*Him?* Tom, are you sure?"

"I'm not sure, no, but it was either him or a bear. You should've seen the fur he left in the front bumper. Hell, I'll take you out there right now."

Jason stood up straight. "No, no, I believe you. If he's outside, I'm not gonna want to go out there until the morning. I've got my AR in the truck, though, so if we do go out there we gotta grab it."

"Fat load of good it does out there," Tom said.

"Well then let's go get it," he replied.

As Jason bent down to get his truck key from his pocket, they were startled by a sharp thudding sound from the other room. "The children!" Elise exclaimed. "I should go check on that."

"I'm coming with," said Tom, and he gave Isabel a squeeze before following his sister-in-law into the other room.

In the living room, the children were pooled together in a makeshift nest of blankets and sleeping bags on the floor. Whatever the sound had been, it hadn't woken them up. Tom turned his phone flashlight on and swept it around the room, but didn't see anything out of place.

"That's weird," he said. "There's nothing out of..."

There was another sharp thump, so loud that it made Tom jump and drop his phone, the flashlight clattering to the ground and plunging them into darkness.

"What was that?" Elise sharply hissed.

"It was outside," whispered Tom. "Get down."

They both dropped to their knees, Tom grabbing his phone and turned his flashlight off in the process. Tom transferred his attention to the giant framed window in the center of the living room, under which all the children were sleeping. "It's him," he explained. "He did this same thing to the Molinas when we were kids. Sheriff Callahan said that's why they moved out so suddenly." Another rock thudded against the side of the house. "We gotta draw him away before he breaks this window."

Jason stuck his head into the room. "What's going on?" He asked. "Is everyone okay?"

"He's outside," both Elise and Tom whispered in unison.

Jason swore silently. "With my fucking AR. Do you have a weapon, Tom?"

"No," he said. "I flew, and we didn't check any luggage."

Elise pointed towards the kitchen. "I have my twenty-two. It's in my purse on the counter by the stove."

Jason sighed. A twenty-two wasn't much, but it was something. He'd faced off with the sasquatch armed with an air-rifle when he was a kid. "That'll have to work. I'm going to go get my AR. Stay here."

"What? No!" Elise shouted after him.

Something clattered against the window, but the glass remained intact. Both Tom and Elise ducked instinctively. Tom heard talking in the kitchen, then the sound of the old sliding-glass backdoor opening and shutting.

"He's gonna get himself killed," Tom groaned.

The barrage of thrown items against the house stopped almost as soon as Jason shut the back door. Tom, Elise, and Isabel waited in the living room in silence for what seemed like a year, the slumbering children's snoozes and the ticking of a clock the only sounds for miles around. Suddenly, there was another crashing noise near the back of the house. Tom heard Jason yell outside, followed by four sharp gunshots from the twenty-two - POP! POP! POP! POP!

Elise yelped in fear, causing the children to stir. There was a horrendous, eerie howling noise outside, like that of a gigantic coyote, and then a sound like an automobile accident, and then... silence.

Without any idea of the whereabouts of his brother or the monster, Tom suddenly became incredibly aware of the fact that the only two known firearms on the property were both now outside. He rushed across the room, and seized a poker from the fireplace. “Stay right there!” He barked towards the women, and he rushed out the back door after Jason.

Outside it was pitch black save the yellow glow of the back porch light. “Jason!” Tom called for his brother but received no reply. Brandishing the fireplace poker at the darkness, he took two steps off the porch and called again. “Jason!”

An owl screeched somewhere in the forest, making Tom jump, but the forest was otherwise silent. Tom fumbled in his pocket for his phone, before realizing he had left it inside. He ran out into the darkness around the house, seeing only by the light streaming from the windows, and into the front yard.

In the driveway, he could see his rental Mitsubishi had been moved from where it was parked. The gravel of the driveway was thrown up and disturbed, and rocks littered the front yard. On the far end of the parking area in the yard lay Jason’s truck, turned over on its side with the back window broken out. The Mitsubishi was upside-down against it, crumpled like a beer-can on a frat-boy’s forehead. Shattered glass sparkled in the light from the house all around the two vehicles. A small black item lay about twenty feet from the truck between it and Tom, and Tom made his way over to it still brandishing his fireplace poker. He picked up the item and turned it over in his hands- the twenty-two, still hot from firing, that had failed to protect his brother.

## Chapter Nine

"Goddamnit!"

The screen door slammed as Alice entered the house. She was covered in mud and chicken shit, but she beelined for the master bathroom. Tom noticed that she was bleeding from her arm. "Are you okay, mom?" He asked.

"It's just a cut, baby," she responded. "Get me the first aid kit, would you?"

Tom hopped up from the couch where he had been watching the television and ran to the kitchen. He flung open the cabinet underneath the sink and rummaged around until he procured the bright red plastic bin that contained the first aid kit. Holding it triumphantly out from his body, he ran back to his mother who had made her way to the restroom. Handing the first aid kit to her, he commented, "that sure is a lot of blood."

"Oh, it's not all mine," Alice said, running her arm under cold water. "I think we had a visitor in the chicken coop last night."

Tom grimaced. "Raccoon?"

Alice shook her head. "They don't live this far north. I'm thinking lynx or fox. Or coyote. Or maybe bear, even. Definitely something bigger than a raccoon."

Tom's blood ran cold. His mind immediately went to the thing that he and Jason had encountered in the woods last fall, to the polaroid pictures and cast of its tracks hidden behind the side of the top dresser drawer in his bedroom. He didn't speak as his mother continued.

"I swear, you've gotta build those things like a tank to keep the animals out of them out here. The Adamses down the road had a bear in their trash last week. I'll bet it's the same one."

"Probably," Tom muttered.

Alice looked up from her injury, now obviously just a scratch on her arm. Most of the blood had been the chickens'. "Tom, baby, what's the matter?"

Tom's voice dropped, and he couldn't even look his mother in the eye. "Do you think that Harmony…" He didn't finish the sentence.

"Tom, don't beat yourself up thinking about that," Alice said, patting her arm dry with one of the bad towels

"You heard what Sheriff Callahan said. There's nothing that we could've done to prevent what happened to your sister. Accidents just… happen sometimes. Especially with wildlife."

*Dad could've not brought her outside,* thought Tom, but he dared not say it. Shifting the blame to his father would only invoke the fury of his mother, after all.

"At any rate, we've got three dead chickens outside. They're still fresh, but they won't be for long. Come on, let's go make use of their meat."

Outside, it was clear where the chicken coop had been accessed. The little wood shack measured about six feet by eight feet, with two of its four sides wrapped by a chicken run framed in with wood and chicken-wire. None of the wood appeared broken, but the chicken-wire had been meticulously peeled back from around the door starting at about seven feet up.

"Awfully tall fox," Tom muttered.

"Or bear," replied Alice. "Just hold it open for me."

Tom stood on his tippy-toes and took the chicken wire delicately so it wouldn't scratch him. He peeled it back far enough for his mother to open the door, and held it in place as she entered the chicken run. She rounded the corner and undid the clasp that held the wall of the coop shut, then lifted it open. Inside, the remaining chickens dodged about uneasily, cooing their concerns to each other. Alice reached into the darkness of the chicken-coop and produced two dead chickens, which she bunched together and held by the neck with one hand - their lifeless bodies dangling limply from her clenched fist, while she fished out a third with her other.

Turning back with her prize, Alice let the chicken-coop slam shut behind her, then used her foot to open the lower door so the birds could freely range about the chicken run. As they slowly poked their reddish-brown heads out into the sunlight, blinking their big orange eyes awkwardly, she made her way to the door where Tom stood. He pulled it back open for her and she brought out the dead fowl, after which he made sure the door shut firmly to keep the remaining birds in place.

Alice handed the single chicken cadaver to Tom, who took it awkwardly. "Here you go, Tom," she said, "it's about time you learned how to pluck one of these."

Tom recognized the chicken immediately. He had never bothered to name his mother's chickens, but he did watch this one from the time she was a newly purchased hatchling. She had always been a boisterous troublemaker, and, Tom thought, frankly a little bit of a bitch. She had bullied the other birds nonstop to the point where some of them were missing feathers, and would have certainly killed them if she had been able to. *Serves you right, you dumb dead bird,* Tom thought.

Alice set down one of the carcasses and launched right into her lesson. "First," she said, "you grip the chicken like this." She held the chicken up by the neck. "Normally, it would be fighting at this point so you would have to mind yourself not to get scratched, but this one isn't. Some people like to shake the bird about, like this..." She violently shook the bird, its body flopping around its neck with a sickening popping noise that made Tom gag a little bit, "but I prefer..." she twisted its head around three hundred and sixty degrees, "...to break its neck in a more controlled way. You don't want it to be painful for the animal."

"Of course," Tom said. "That would be inhumane."

"Well," Alice smirked, "that, and pain releases stress hormones and adrenaline that ruins the taste of the meat. If you want good meat, you've gotta treat the chicken good."

"Tender life, tender meat," Tom mused.

"Exactly." She smiled. "Next, you're going to hold your chicken like this, and slit its throat to drain the blood out." She held the bird upside-down and cut quickly and neatly across its neck, whereupon bright crimson blood began pouring out of its neck. "Hold it away from your body so the blood doesn't get on you." She turned the knife so its blade faced her and offered Tom the handle.

Tom took the knife and pressed it against the dead chicken's throat. Her eyes were shut, but he could imagine her looking at him. "Like… like this?"

"Yes, now nice and quick. Don't cut all the way through, though. You don't want to decapitate her entirely."

Tom brought the knife towards himself quickly, and sliced the chicken's throat open. Hot, oxygenated blood began to pour out and splattered down his pants and onto his shoe, leaving a bright scarlet streak down his leg.

"Hold it out! Hold it out!" Alice said. She grimaced towards her son. "You're making a mess now."

"I'm sorry," Tom said. "It's definitely dead now."

"That's the idea." Alice said. She held the chicken out and looked off into the distance as blood poured into the dust below their feet. "It'll take about two minutes for the blood to drain. After that, it's not chicken the animal anymore."

"It's chicken the food," Tom muttered.

His mother smiled. "That's right, Tom. It's chicken the food."

---

Tom and Jason hadn't traveled more than two hundred feet further down the deerpath when Jason motioned with his hand for Tom to stop. Neither of the boys had spoken - both were too worried about what else might be out in the woods with them, and the sound of ice melting out of the spruce trees sounded like the pitter patter of tiny creatures surrounding them and keeping them on edge. Jason had stopped momentarily before, but Tom noted that this was the first time that he had motioned for both of them to do so.

"What is it?" Tom whispered, breaking the silence.

Jason pointed to the ground ahead of them. In a low, muddy spot on the trail was another footprint, six or so inches wide and about as long as Tom's shin. The water in the edges of it was crystallized into ice, but you could very clearly make out a rounded heel, a long, broad foot surface, and five toes without claw marks.

"That's a big footprint," Tom whispered.

"That's a bigfoot print," Jason corrected him. "Take the picture. I'll keep watch."

Tom pulled the polaroid camera out from his jacket and snapped a picture of the footprint. He waited for the camera to print the photograph, then waved it gently in the air while it developed. His eyes followed the trail from the footprint about four feet further down, where he spotted another footprint.

"Jason! Look!" He whispered, nudging his brother.

"Oh, sweet!" Said Jason. "I read in dad's old Boy Scout handbook how to figure out the height of someone if you have two footprints!" Jason immediately set about measuring the tracks. He measured the first footprint to be sixteen inches long, and confirmed that the tracks were about fifty inches apart, just over four feet. Doing his mathematics out loud, Jason calculated the height of the sasquatch. "...Divided by two is... eighty-nine inches tall. That's just over seven feet."

"That's all?" Tom asked incredulously. "I thought it was a monster, not hairy Shaquille O'neal."

Jason pointed towards the track. "Yeah but look how deep this heel indent is. I'll bet he's four or five hundred pounds, at least."

"At least," Tom repeated, clutching his air rifle. "Definitely going to take eleven pumps of this bad boy. Or I'll pop him once in the eye and you finish him off."

"Tom," Jason said, "I'm not so sure we should continue. We might be in danger."

"Should we give up and cut back towards the house through the woods?" Tom asked. "Or go back the way we came? What if it goes back to the North Gate?"

"What if these tracks aren't that old and we catch up with it?" Jason had a quiver of fear in his voice, and Tom could tell he was really concerned.

"Look," Tom tried to put on an air of bravery, "the northeast corner of the property is about another quarter mile in this direction. From there, it's about half a mile south before you hit the power line path. From there, we'd be able to walk in the open back to the house. If you ask me, that beats trekking back through the woods or back-tracking. We set out to reclaim Harm's Queendom. I say we finish what we've started."

"And if we run into the Bigfoot?" Jason asked.

Tom lifted his air rifle and pumped it. "Twelve pumps now."

---

"No signal," Elise groaned, "of fucking course." She shoved her phone back into her pocket disappointedly.

"Doesn't matter anyways," Isabel said, pointing at Tom's phone where it lay on the ground.

There was a knock on the door, causing everyone to jump.

"Open up! It's me!" Tom's voice called from outside. Elise quickly crossed the room, unlocked the front door, and let Tom in. His eyes were wide with fear, and he was soaked in sweat. In one hand he clutched Elise's twenty-two handgun. His brother's AR-15 rifle dangled limply from the other.

"Where's Jason?" Elise asked, her voice shaking.

"Gone," Tom said. "I think the Sasquatch took him."

Elise teared up and began to cry, while Isabel swore to herself. "Do you think he's..." Isabel couldn't finish.

"Dead?" Tom asked. "I don't think so. I heard him yelling. At least, he was alive when the Sasquatch carried him off."

"We need to get out of here!" Elise cried, stooping to wake the children.

"Can't," said Tom. "Fucking beast threw my car into your truck, then flipped it on it's side. That's what Jace was going for." He lifted his brother's rifle for emphasis. "This was in the truck."

"We need backup," Isabel said. "Who do we know in this area?"

"There is one person we can call," Tom said. "Is there still a functioning landline somewhere in this house?"

---

"It Won't Be Long" by Johnny Paycheck wafted lazily through the hazy bar from tinny speakers the better part of a century old as the bartender polished glasses with a towel to try and look busy. It was a weeknight, and business had been slow. In fact, right this moment the only other person in the bar was Andrew Callahan, former sheriff and local kooky old man. The bartender considered himself good friends with Mr. Callahan, who spent pretty much every evening in his establishment as it was reportedly the best of three bars in the vicinity of Skitooa, Alaska, and since it wasn't ski season or elk season there really wasn't anyone else around to sell liquor to, so he considered him a pretty good customer as well.

Suddenly, the phone rang, startling the bartender. It was 2020, and frankly the bartender hadn't used a landline in so long that he had forgotten they existed, much less that they had one in his little dive bar. Still, he set down the glass he had now overpolished, dug the phone out from under a stack of papers and discarded towels behind the barback, and picked up the receiver.

"Elmo's Tavern, Barry speaking," the bartender said. "Uh huh. Who's this?" A pause, then "Sure, I'll tell him."

The bartender hung up the phone, then crossed the bar again to the old man who was sipping a glass of water and humming along to the music faintly playing. "Hey, Sheriff," Barry said. "Tom Carlini just called, says he needs your help at the homestead. Says it's an emergency."

Andrew Callahan, it should be mentioned, had led a long and full life. The son of a war hero, Andrew had been born while his father was overseas fighting nazis in 1942. He served in Vietnam, racking up a reputation as an expert outdoorsman and jungle navigator, and learning well how to jerry-rig broken equipment that Uncle Sam had sent with you into hell to get the most out of it. After the war, his best friend had decided to disappear into the Alaskan wilderness to escape the society he considered to have failed him, so Callahan had gone to Alaska with him, bought some land near Susitna, built himself a little cabin, and practically disappeared with him.

The problem was, Andrew Callahan loved Alaska. He loved the Met-Su. He loved the mountains and the valleys and the rivers that met in tumbling whitewater rapids to plummet half a mile to the Pacific Ocean below. He loved the lodgepole pines stretching into the heavens, and he even loved the tourists who would flock northward to simultaneously enjoy and tarnish the Great Outdoors of the Last Frontier. He ended up putting his veteran skills to work and gaining employment as a deputy with the Met-Su Sheriff Department.

From there, Andrew worked up the ranks until the 1988 election, when he ran for - and won - the position of Sheriff. Andrew worked as Sheriff for ten years, during which he responded to the 1992 disappearance of Harmony Carlini. It was during this time that he discovered the existence of sasquatches as a species, and the existence of the Met-Su Monster in particular. It was a male, around fifty or sixty years old, and it was mean. Quite frankly, it was the most dangerous animal that Andrew Callahan had ever encountered, human or otherwise, and he'd encountered killer bears, wolves, and men. After Andrew Callahan resigned from his position of Sheriff, he devoted his life to tracking the beast and trying to trap and kill it.

Of course, Tom Carlini didn't know that second part when he called. He just figured that the old man was a close friend of his father's, had a four wheel drive truck, and a few guns, but it was definitely a happy accident.

---

Jason led Tom to the northwest corner of the property, now clutching Nathan's rifle with both hands. Tom brought up the rear, warily watching in all directions. The sun had melted most of the snow now, and the pitter-patter of falling water had more or less stopped, but as the forest woke up in the sunlight it had been replaced with the sound of small animals scurrying about the forest floor. Any animal moving through the leaf detritus always sounds much larger than it actually is, and every squirrel and rabbit nearly made Tom jump out of his shoes.

They reached the point in the northwestern boundary of the property where the deer-path moved through the barbed-wire fence and into the untamed wild beyond, and turned to cut south. Here, the going would get much rougher - they would be moving through untrailed woodland for about half a mile until they linked up with the clear-cut path where the telephone line bisected the forest. Tom checked again to ensure that his air rifle was still loaded and ready to go, then looked towards Jason and asked, "are you ready?"

Jason shrugged. "Ready as I'll ever be." He took a deep breath, drew his rifle closer to him, and stepped off the path.

Off the trail, the mood of the forest shifted. Even a few feet from the deer-path, it suddenly felt like deep wilderness. Tom and Jason tensed up, knowing that they were now trespassers in a wild that did not belong to them. They were on the sasquatch's turf now. Despite the rising sun the woods felt like they were growing darker and more menacing by the minute as the snow on the ground started melting and stopped reflecting glittering, magical light everywhere.

"Jason?" Tom asked.

"Yeah, Tom?" He replied, barely over a whisper.

"Do you think the sasquatch is still on our property?"

Jason glanced away from his brother, into the woods. "I don't know, Tom."

Tom kicked at the forest floor a little as he walked, leaving a streak of discarded orange spruce needles exposed under the glittering snow. “Do you think he’s watching us? Right now?”

This time, Jason’s voice quivered a little bit. “I don’t know, Tom.”

“Do you think...” He didn’t want to vocalize it - not that he had to, they were both thinking it. “Do you think he got Harmony?”

“I don’t know, Tom.” Jason said again, a tinge of hopelessness this time. Tom figured it was in their best interest to be quiet, hoping that if they did encounter the bigfoot they could simply slip by it unnoticed.

They pressed on further into the woods. This part of the fenceline wasn’t as well kept as the fenceline at the front of the property, probably because there was little chance of human trespassers coming across it since the next building in this direction was the little old logging cabin four miles away. Back when the boys used to play Kingdoms, before Harmony disappeared, the area past the eastern fence used to be called the “wildlands”. Nobody really ever laid claim to the wildlands, they were just there. They never really ventured that far, assuming it to be full of wolves and grizzly bears and all manner of other things. Now, as they walked along the eastern fence, Tom kept peering over his shoulder and into the wildlands. He figured the worst time to be attacked by a pack of wolves would be while being hunted by a sasquatch. Tom voiced his concerns to Jason, but Jason just said to keep his voice down and keep moving.

There was the sound of crashing brush somewhere to the boys' right, back on their property. They froze, listening for another hint. Jason lowered the rifle from his shoulder and pointed it in the direction of the noise. Tom could see his lips moving, saying, repeating, praying, "please be a caribou". The woods were too dense to see what had made the noise, but they could still hear it scuttling around in the undergrowth, and it sounded very large. Tom and Jason stood frozen in fear for a minute, until they felt reasonably sure that the potential bigfoot was moving away from them, then Jason gestured for Tom to continue forward towards the power lines, and the creek that lay just beyond them. They would ultimately have to head back to the right to get to the relative safety of the house, but it made sense to try and put the creek bed between them and the creature.

## Chapter Ten

Tom wasn't sure what compelled him to take his father's pickup truck into town. The ladies had sent him to get a few grocery items for their stay, about a week past the funeral, and honestly it gave him an excuse to get away from Jason for a while. He loved his brother, but Jason was a lot for multiple consecutive days. He could've driven his own rental car, but decided that for the sake of reliving the good ol' days it was best to drive the old blue Chevy into Talkeetna. Now, he sat in the parking lot of Nagley's Grocery, breathing in the smell of his late father's work truck and letting himself slip deep into thought.

A sharp rapping on the truck's window broke Tom's trance. He turned to see a short man, on the border between middle-aged and elderly, peering at him through aviator sunglasses. The man had an unkempt beard and wore a tan button-up with the top three buttons undone, displaying a hairy chest bronzed by the sun.

"I'm sorry," Tom said. He was about to say that he didn't have any money but the man cut him off before he had the chance.

"Thomas? Thomas Carlini? Is that you?"

Tom squinted at the man. Where could he possibly know him from?

"Thomas Carlini! It's me, Andrew Callahan!"

Something clicked in Tom's mind. Sheriff Callahan! Of course! Almost a decade since Tom had last seen the man, he had definitely aged, as people who spend all their time outdoors tend to do. Tom rolled the window down.

"Sheriff! What are you doing here?"

Callahan tugged at his shirt, showing off the lack of a badge. "Retired. You can call me Andrew now, or Mr. Callahan if you prefer. I recognized your dad's truck. I am so sorry for your loss."

"Yeah," Tom sighed, "well, you can't live forever, I suppose."

"He died doing what he loved, son," Callahan said. "Outdoors in the woods, breathing fresh air. Take comfort in that. Far too many people these days die in germ-riddled hospitals or in stuffy old folks' homes." He paused a second to reflect. "How's your ma holding up?"

Tom shrugged. "One day at a time, I suppose. How 'bout Dingo? He being a good boy for you?"

The former sheriff nodded in the affirmative. Dingo had never been a family dog, and it just made sense for him to hold onto him since they'd spent more time in the field together than Dingo had ever spent at the Carlini residence.

"You must be freezing!" Tom exclaimed, politely. "I was just about to go in to get some groceries. Care to join me?"

Callahan raised his own grocery bag. "I should really drop these off to the missus. Where are you staying? I can swing by later."

"We're staying at the property. All of us are."

"The property. Of course." The old man looked up towards the sun, checking the time by holding his fingers outstretched against the horizon. "When you get back, tell your mom and your brother to expect company around eight o' clock." He grinned and extended his hand through the truck window. "It was great to see you, Thomas."

Tom shook his hand. "Of course. Glad to see a friendly face."

Callahan nodded, then shot Tom a fleeting look of sympathy. He broke the handshake, turned, and walked to his truck.

Tom sat back to think. Prior to that, the last time he had spoken to Callahan was before the funeral. He hadn't shown up. The trauma of his father's death was far too fresh, and there was always paperwork to be done. Instead, he had called a few days prior before Tom had left the Lower 48 to make the trek back to offer his condolences. "Your father was a good man," he had said. "I owe him my life." At the time, Tom had been angry. Angry at God, the universe, the bear, whoever. Why did the bear have to take his father and not Callahan? But time heals all wounds, and Tom had forgiven the old man, even if he maybe hadn't forgiven himself.

---

Neither of the Carlini boys had spoken in at least five minutes as they trekked through the forest. Conifer needles and yellowed aspen-leaves made up a dense carpet across the forest floor, and Tom and Jason were careful to lift their feet between steps and step on top of the detritus which padded their steps and helped them remain quiet, blending in with the pitter-patter of melting snow all around them. Tom had realized he was breathing heavily, and tried to slow his breath to quiet down as he followed Jason south towards the power lines.

"Are you sure this is the right way?" Tom whispered to his brother.

"We're still inside the property," Jason responded. He pointed at the barbed wire fence at the edge of the property, now some thirty feet away through the trees. "As long as that fence is on our left, we're going the right direction."

The boys hadn't heard the monster for a while now, but Tom could feel its eyes on the back of his head. It was an uneasy feeling, being watched, and Tom didn't know what the beast was capable of. Neither of them had actually gotten a glimpse at the animal, and Tom had tried his hardest to rationalize it as just a bear, but honestly a bear wasn't that much less scary for two boys to encounter while alone in the woods. At this point, their only real chance was getting back out of the forest and into the house.

They reached the power line cutout and stumbled out of the woods into the open air. They couldn't quite see the house from here, as there was a foothill between it and their position, but Tom felt a little better knowing that there was a straight-shot towards the house and, at the very least, if they had to discharge a firearm their parents would likely be able to hear them. He even forgot for a moment how much trouble they would be in if his father woke up and discovered that his hunting rifle had been stolen. The boys took a second to catch their breath, then headed west back towards the house.

The entire journey up the cutout, Tom still felt eyes on the back of his head. As they crested the foothill and got their glimpse of the house in the distance, smoke rising gently out of the chimney about a quarter mile away telling them that their father had definitely been up by now at least for long enough to stoke last night's fire, they heard the familiar crashing in the undergrowth in the forest to their right. Peering into the dark woods, they still couldn't see anything, but it was apparent to them that the beast was getting closer. As they descended down the hill towards the ravine below, the crashing only got louder and louder. Tom was watching the forest, terrified, but Jason's head remained straight. He remained focused on getting back to the house.

"If we come across it," Jason said to Tom, "you know our best chance of survival isn't shooting it, right?"

"It isn't?" Tom asked.

He shook his head. "No, that's not what dad taught me. If you come across a wild animal, you're supposed to make yourself look big and make a lot of noise. The gun might be good for making noise for sure, but shooting it might make it mad. We want to try and scare it off first."

"Scare it off," Tom repeated. "How do we do that?"

"Yell," he shrugged, "puff your shoulders up, hold your arms out, maybe even throw stuff at it. Anything to make it too scared to fight us. If it comes down to a one on one fight and the rifle doesn't do its job, we don't stand a chance."

Tom nodded. He understood perfectly what his brother was saying. They were in very real danger as long as they were the object of the sasquatch's attention. The two descended the foot-hill towards the ravine in silence, watching the forest keenly every time they heard a snapping twig or the sound of shuffling leaf-litter.

It was about another half-mile before the boys made it to the ravine. During the spring, when the snow melted off the surrounding mountains and into the Talkeetna River, the ravine became a creek - roaring whitewater during the earliest days of the thaw, slowing to a gentle flow during the summer and drying up in the fall before entering hibernation again for the winter. Now, it was mostly dry, with a deep muddy rut running through the center. The last trickle had disappeared with the morning's frost. This left a ditch some ten feet across and ten feet deep, carving the Carlini property in half, the bottom layered in loam and decaying tree-litter carried from upstream and deposited here. The power line went over the ravine with ease, but it would be a more daunting obstacle for the boys.

"You reckon we should take the creek down to the road that goes to the swimmin' hole?" Tom asked his brother.

"Why?" Jason responded.

Tom shrugged. "It's low down. It'd be harder for the bigfoot to see us down there."

Jason shook his head. "Yeah, and harder for us to see him. No, we jump it. It gets wider a ways up ahead, and I'd like to have it between us and him. We can still get him with the guns, but he won't be able to get us."

"Not without a gun anyways," Tom joked, but he was still worried. The seven foot tall beast could still probably jump pretty far. Tom knew for a fact that Shaq could jump the creek, but it might still work to put their minds at ease just a little bit. Plus, his brother was right. It got wider downstream, and a twenty foot ravine was better than a ten foot one. "Alright," he sighed. "Well, let's do it."

Jason nodded, and handed the rifle to his brother. "Now it's gonna be a long jump, so watch me and then do exactly as I do, okay?" Tom nodded. Jason backed up a ways, then took a running start. Tom held his breath as his brother launched himself into the air, landed on the other side, and tucked into a somersault to dispel his excess kinetic energy. He reached out his hands and called for Tom to toss him the rifle.

Tom opened up the action on the rifle and released the chambered round, then tossed the gun across the ravine. Jason caught it, and gestured again. Tom tossed the cartridge, which landed near Jason's feet. He stooped down and picked it up, wiped it off, and loaded it back into the rifle. He held out his hands again. "Alright, now the air rifle!"

"Are you sure?" Tom asked. "What if the sasquatch gets me? I don't want to be caught on this side without protection."

"You won't be," Jason assured him. "I've got the rifle ready to go over here. I could peg him for you."

Tom took a deep breath, then nodded and tossed the rifle over. The air rifle wasn't as heavy as the real rifle, however, and caught the wind much more easily. Tom and Jason both audibly gasped as it failed to clear the ravine, knocked off the far side, fired with a loud "*pop!*", and clattered down into the ditch.

"Goddamnit," Tom swore.

"What did you do?" Asked Jason.

"I-I- I don't know," Tom stuttered. "I'll just climb in and get it. I wasn't going to make the jump anyways."

From the forest came a sharp shout, deep and guttural. It sounded almost human, like the apes he'd seen once at the zoo. Tom's blood ran cold. He knew now for certain that they weren't dealing with a bear.

"Hurry!" Jason called, not even trying to be quiet anymore. The sasquatch definitely knew where they were.

Tom dropped to the ground and swung his legs over the ravine. He knew that ten feet wasn't as far down as it seemed, but he made the mistake of looking down and froze in place. "Tom!" Jason yelled. "Drop!"

Tom shook himself free from his trance and shoved off of the ledge with his arms. For a moment he dangled freely in the air, legs kicking back and forth, before he hit the ground with a sharp cry.

"Are you okay, Tom?" Jason's face peeked over the ravine.

Tom nodded. "I think I rolled my ankle, but I'll be okay!"

"Good, now get the gun!"

There was another cry from the forest, this one less sharp and more like the sound of a very large man crying out in anger. It sounded like it was getting closer. Tom picked himself up and crossed the ravine to where his gun was laying in the leaf-litter at the bottom. He plucked it up off the ground, and -

Something lit up in the loam, flashing red and white. Tom froze. "Jason?"

"What?" His brother asked from above. "What is it?"

"When Harm disappeared," Tom asked, "what shoes was she wearing?"

"Uh," Jason thought for a minute. "It was on the poster. Last seen wearing… pink pajamas with light-up sneakers."

Tom stooped down again and plunged his hand into the loam, bringing up the object which he had kicked - a muddied white children's sneaker, with LED lights sparkling in the heel as he moved it.

Tom's eyes welled up with tears as he cradled the light-up sneaker in his arms. They had never found any remains of Harmony, and he knew that, logically, him finding the sneaker likely meant that the rest of her was probably nearby. They had played in this section of the woods since her disappearance, even following the ravine down to the swimming hole on more than one occasion. The thought that they could've been walking over his baby sister's remains made Tom sick to his stomach.

"Tom!" Jason hissed from above. "What's taking you so long?"

"We've been childish," Tom replied in a low whisper.

"What?" Jason asked, peering over the edge of the ravine. He saw his brother solemnly cradling his sister's shoe and froze.

"Childish," Tom repeated himself. "To think that she was just gone. That she disappeared without a trace, just into thin air. Jason, she was killed. She felt fear and pain and was killed by that thing - no, that monster in the woods."

Jason swung his feet over the side of the ravine and skidded down to the bottom, where he knelt beside his brother and gently took the shoe from his hands. "Come on, Tom, let's go. The monster's close. We have to move."

Tom looked at his brother with watering eyes. "What if she's here?" he asked.

"What if?" Jason said. "Tom, we can come back with the sheriff and with dogs and a search party when it's safe. Right now, unless we want to join her we need to go."

Tom started to shake his head, but a barking yell from the creature somewhere in the forest to their east shook him back to his senses. He picked himself up, shouldered his air rifle, took a deep breath, and nodded.

"You're right," he replied. "If we don't get moving, they'll… they'll find three bodies in this gully, won't they?"

Jason rose to his feet, trying not to let the grim thought set in too hard. "Attaboy. Think you can climb back out of here?"

Tom nodded. "If you can give me a boost."

"Sure thing. Then I'll toss up the guns and you hold onto them and keep an eye out until I get up there, capiche?"

Nodding again, Tom stuffed the shoe into his pocket for safekeeping. Jason pressed himself back-first against the gully wall and held out his hands at waist height for Tom, who took his brother by the shoulders and placed his left foot in his hands. Jason lifted Tom up with a grunt of effort, and Tom grabbed the ledge at the top of the gully. He pulled himself up and onto solid ground, nearly kicking his brother in the face in the process. He then reached down and took the firearms from his brother - first the bolt-action rifle and then his own less-lethal air rifle, then rose to his feet and looked towards the woods in the direction of the sasquatch while his brother scrambled up the ravine's crumbling wall.

Once both boys were safely out of the ravine, they paused to think. "The dirt road isn't far from here," Jason said. "It might be better than the wire-trail."

From there, it would be a clean straight-shot home, and they figured that the sasquatch would have the least chance of messing with them on the road, if you could call it a road. In the meantime, they wanted to put as much distance between them and the creature as possible, and the ravine got deeper and wider the further southwest you went along it.

## Chapter Eleven

A car door slammed shut outside the house. Still clutching his brother's rifle, Tom peeked out the window between the blinds and saw Andrew Callahan's K10 Blazer parked outside, the faded paint oddly preserved on the doors where decals once read "MATANUSKA-SUSITNA BOROUGH SHERIFF'S DEPARTMENT", so the letters were still legible in the negative all these years later if you squinted. The old man was making his way to the house, gripping a carbine rifle in either hand. *Good,* Tom thought, *he brought more firepower.*

Callahan knocked on the front door, and Isabel went to let him in. "Quiet," she said as soon as she opened the door. "Mom and the children are sleeping and we don't want to wake them."

Callahan held a single finger to his lips to indicate that he'd be quiet. His face had aged more since Tom had last seen him two decades prior. His skin was drawn taught across his face, leathered with years of sunlight and creased with smile lines, hidden under a light wiry beard that wasn't quite as disheveled as it had been twenty years prior. He'd also lost the last of the hair off the top of his head, but what was left around the sides stuck out wildly like straw. Despite his age, he still had a boyish charm to him. Isabel stood aside and let him inside, then gently closed the door behind her to ensure that the screen door wouldn't slam. "Quite a night, isn't it?" He muttered.

Tom skipped any pleasantries. "Do you think my brother's alright, Sheriff?"

"Please," Callahan chuckled. "I'm no sheriff. Not anymore. Just call me Callahan." He sniffled a little bit. "Your brother's probably still alive, if that's what you're asking. As much as this sasquatch likes to cause trouble, he's not known for killing." His eyes shifted, then his gaze dropped to meet the floor for a moment. "Not right away, anyhow."

"This… this sasquatch?" Elise asked.

"Oh, sure, this sasquatch. I've been watching him ever since your sister disappeared. There are others, true, but he's the only one that ever causes trouble."

Tom gulped. "You mean it's the same one that…"

Callahan nodded, not needing Tom to finish his sentence. "The very same one. How would you like to avenge your sister tonight, Thomas?"

Thomas nodded, but couldn't get out any words. He would have very much liked to avenge his sister, even if it wouldn't necessarily bring her back.

"Good, good," Callahan smiled. "Then it's settled. Tonight, we're killing the Mat-Su Monster."

---

It wasn't five more minutes of travel down the northern rim of the ravine when the boys heard the Sasquatch yelling again. This time it definitely sounded closer and angrier, and they could tell that it had succeeded in crossing the ravine. The boys decided it was best to re-cross the gulch again and try to keep it between them and the beast. They found a decent crossing point and eased their way down the steep, sandy side, crossed the gulch, and climbed up the sheer southern wall using a series of tree roots. Once they were up, Jason took the rifle and shot three rounds - one into each root. The sound of the rifle was deafening, and the boys knew that their parents could probably hear it from the house, but encumbering the sasquatch's pursuit of them was more important at the moment.

The boys gathered themselves and continued to the west. After a few more minutes, Tom suddenly got the now-familiar feeling that he was being watched. Keeping an eye on the forest across the gully, he could see a large mass moving in the shadows. "Jason," Tom whispered, "he's right across there. He's watching us."

"We're gonna have to get past him to get home," Jason responded, making Tom's heart drop into his stomach.

"Make ourselves look big and scary when the time comes?" Tom asked his brother.

Jason nodded. "When the time comes."

The sun was nearly overhead now, and the snow was melting quickly. Whereas the boys had previously been able to make out various tracks left by birds, squirrels, foxes, and deer, all that was left now were round indentations in the slush on the forest floor. Tom was glad that he had gotten polaroids of the tracks, and was eager to return to the North Gate to gather his footprint cast. He felt nobody would believe their tales of a monster in the forest without hard evidence. It occurred to him that, were the beast smart enough, it would also be capable of tracking their footprints through the snow, but that the rising sun would be melting them as well. He supposed it gave them at least some small level of advantage.

By the time the boys reached the little wooden bridge where the road to the hunting-cabin and swimming-hole crossed the ravine, they hadn't heard or seen the beast in several minutes. Its putrid odor, which hung in the air like a skunk, had even begun to fade. They hoped that it had lost interest in them as they approached the homestead and left them alone, but they weren't letting their guard down. Jason held his finger up to his lip to tell Tom to remain absolutely silent until they made it back to the house, and Tom nodded in agreement. The boys crossed the bridge and warily and briskly set off northwards up the double-track road towards the house.

Suddenly, the sasquatch got wind of them again. It let out a grunt somewhere to their left, and they heard it picking up speed across the forest floor. Knowing they were still being followed, the boys increased their pace from a brisk walk to a light jog, clutching their weapons tightly to their chests. They crested the final foothill before the homestead and clearly saw the house, lights on and smoke pouring out of the chimney. They could even see their mother out by the chicken-coop, clearly engaged in Jason's chores which he had neglected to do before striking out. The boys broke out into an all-out sprint, racing the creature to safety. Looking to his right, Tom could see it running through the woods on two feet, shaggy orangish-brown fur catching the sunlight, its head a mass of tangled hair with no discernable facial features from a distance of twenty or so yards, hulking eight feet tall or higher. Tom was so terrified he couldn't make a sound - all he could do was keep running.

Jason stumbled and fell to his knee, nearly losing his grip on his weapon. Tom shouted in fear as the beast turned and began to bear down on the boys. Jason raised the rifle and fired a single shot in its direction, which exploded harmlessly in a tree-trunk behind it. Tom stopped and raised his air-rifle, taking more time to aim than his brother had, and unleashed a shot with a pop! The pellet-gun was once again cocked with eleven pumps, and the pellet hit the beast in the face. It let out a monstrous, bellowing roar of pain, and turned and disappeared into the forest.

At the homestead several hundred feet away, Alice Carlini heard the gunshots and the roar, and rushed out of the chicken-coop and towards the woods. “Tom!” She called. “Jason! Are you out there?”

“We’re here, mom!” Jason hollered back, rising to his feet. “Something attacked us but we’re here and we’re safe!” Both boys broke out into a run and closed the final four hundred feet to the homestead without hazarding a glance over their shoulders lest the beast be in pursuit. As they entered the clearing, Jason dropped the hunting rifle, but Tom clutched onto his Daisy for dear life. Jason ran to his mother and embraced her. “We’re safe, we’re safe!” He kept repeating the words, not sure whether he was more trying to convince Alice or himself. “We’re safe. We’re safe.”

“What the hell were you doing out there?” Alice said. She was trying to not sound like she was scolding the boys, as she was more concerned than anything.

"We were reclaiming Harm's Queendom, mom." Tom said. "We walked the perimeter but got chased off by a monster. And mom..." He produced the light-up sneaker from his pocket. "And we found this."

---

The mood after Nathan Carlini's memorial service was friendly, if gloomy. A thick air of sorrow filled the homestead, but everyone more or less agreed that it was good to see each other even under such bleak circumstances. Family and neighbors gathered together to mourn the loss of Nathan, who was something of a pillar of the community. Notably absent was Sheriff Callahan, who was in the hospital recovering from the same hunting accident that had taken his partner's life. Some of the more extended family left immediately after the service, and come sundown all that remained at the property were the widow Alice, her two surviving sons Tom and Jason, Tom's wife Isabel, and Jason's girlfriend Elise.

Nathan's ashes had been buried near the north end of the property line next to his daughter's remains, in what was quickly becoming the family plot. His service revolver, issued to him by Alaska Parks And Wildlife which he had been a loyal servant to for many years, was buried with him. A quarter mile away up the driveway, his immediate family sat around a blazing fireplace sharing their fondest memories of him.

The hour began to draw late. Alice stretched and yawned, excused herself, and retreated to spend her first night alone in her marital bed. The adult Carlini children decided among themselves that they didn't want to try to sleep in their childhood beds, and determined that the best alternative would be to hike down to the hunting-cabin half a mile to the south and camp out.

Jason took his twenty-two caliber pistol for protection, and the four slipped out the backdoor quietly so as to not wake their mother and headed off into the night. A golden-silver orb of a full moon lit the forest in a pale glow, so they were able to see their way without need for flashlights. Once they were a safe distance away from the house as to where their voices wouldn't carry and risk waking their tired, grieving mother, they began talking and joking amongst themselves.

Tom, however, didn't quite seem as jovial as the other three. Jason took notice of this and drew back behind the girls with his brother. "Tom?" He asked quietly. "Is there something wrong?"

"It's just…" Tom started, then paused to think over his words, "the last time we were out here in these woods outside of daylight hours, He was there."

Jason scoffed a little. "Most of the time he was following us, it was light out. I don't think he's nocturnal."

"Why wouldn't he be?" Tom asked.

"Did you notice his eyes? When he stood up straight watching you?"

Tom thought back to that morning ten years prior. He hadn't seen eyes on the creature's head, nor had he seen a distinct neck. Just a mass of fur. "No," he said.

"And why not?" Jason asked. Tom shrugged, so Jason answered his own question. "No eyeshine, Tom. Any creature that can see in the dark is going to have eyeshine. He didn't. Thus he can't see in the dark, thus he probably isn't awake."

Tom shrugged. What his brother was saying seemed to line up with his knowledge of biology. "That makes sense."

"Catch up," Jason said, picking up his pace to rejoin the girls. "We'll be fine."

Sure enough, the three Carlinis and one soon-to-be made it to the hunting cabin without incident. The door wasn't locked - it's common courtesy in the country's more northern regions to leave hunting cabins unlocked so that a hunter or traveller caught in a snowstorm might have a safe place to ride it out without freezing to death - and Jason opened it up and beckoned the others inside. They lit their flashlights and set about getting the cabin ready for the night. Tom brought some firewood in from the shed, checking it carefully for spiders first, and lit a fire in the hearth illuminating the cabin. It was a small structure, consisting of two rooms. The main room served as living room, dining room, and kitchen, with a propane camp-stove, a sink fed by the spring under the cabin, and a table for food preparation and eating. The living room half of the room had a battered loveseat and two comfortable reading chairs all arranged in a semicircle around the hearth. Hunting trophies lined the walls, and above the mantle in a sort of place of honor was an ancient wood-axe, which Nathan Carlini had used to clear the land that the cabin now sat on twenty years prior. In the back room there were two bunk-beds for four beds total and a wardrobe which contained bedding. The girls went into the back room to prepare the beds while Tom tended to the fire and Jason, armed with his twenty-two, swept the cabin and made sure there were no unwanted intruders taking up residence, human or otherwise.

Once the cabin was made up to their liking, the Carlinis settled down in the living room around the fire to continue their storytelling and joking. During a lull in the conversation, Isabel whispered to Tom, “Do you think we'll see him tonight?”

“See who?” Elise asked curiously.

Tom and Jason went silent, glancing at each other. Isabel leaned forward and whispered, “the sasquatch.”

Elise laughed, thinking that it was a joke, but her smile faded when she saw the look on the boys' faces. “You're serious?”

Tom nodded. “He's out here. And he's vicious.”

Though she didn't believe them at first, the look on both brothers' faces told Elise that they weren't lying. A chill went down her spine as her mind raced to make the connection before the boys told her.

"I haven't seen him since I was a child," Jason said somberly.

"Mmhmm," Tom said, "and that's not even the worst part."

"Tell us," Elise said.

"He was the one who abducted Harmony."

There was a scream off in the distance, like a woman being murdered. Both of the girls in the cabin shrieked. Even Tom was unnerved, but Jason just looked out towards the window.

"What the fuck was that?" Elise exclaimed.

"That was a mountain lion," Jason said. "They're not this far north often but we do get them from time to time."

Isabel jumped up and ran to the door, sliding the deadbolt into place. "No. No no no no no. I am not dealing with a mountain lion tonight."

"The mountain lion isn't the one we should be worried about," Jason said. "It can't get in here."

"That's enough, Jason," said Tom. "Stop fucking with them. Nothing is getting in here tonight."

The mountain lion screamed again off in the distance, a haunting wail like a woman being torn asunder. Elise shuddered. "I wish she would shut up."

"She's searching for a mate," Tom said. "Unless you're a male mountain lion, she's not interested in you."

Elise sat down in one of the chairs around the fireplace. "Good. Let's keep it that way. Anyone have a deck of cards? Did we bring any booze?"

Jason produced a flask from his pocket and passed it to his girlfriend. "No cards, but I think there's a checkerboard around here somewhere. Tom, see if you can't find it."

"Aye aye, captain," Tom groaned sarcastically, and set about searching for the game set.

The mountain lion shrieked again. Tom thought it sounded like it was getting closer. Elise groaned again, and Jason took the flask from her and took a swig. Tom located the checkerboard on top of the otherwise empty bookshelf and handed it to Elise, who slumped out of the chair and onto the floor in front of the fireplace. "Awesome," she said, "now who's playing me?"

"I guess that's me," Tom said, sitting criss-cross across from her as she set up the board. "Who wants to play winner?"

"Not it," Jason mumbled as he took a swig from his flask. He pulled a face and swallowed with an exaggerated gasping sound.

"I guess that means me," Isabel said, leaning forward to watch the game.

The mountain lion screamed again. It was definitely getting closer to the house. Elise shuddered a little bit.

Then, a sound followed the mountain lion. It was a familiar yelling sound, almost a howl, eerily human but animalistic and raw. Everyone in the cabin froze, and Tom's blood ran cold.

"What was that?" Elise whispered.

Tom and Jason looked at each other and both muttered an answer together.

"Him."

## Chapter Twelve

The boys relayed the entire story of what had happened to them that morning to their mother, using the photographs of the footprints and the light-up sneaker as evidence. Tom wished that he had the presence of mind to photograph the beast as it chased them through the woods, but knew that he couldn't blame himself for that failure. Alice knew better than to disbelieve her children, and though she was skeptical concerning the nature of the beast, she figured it was best to call the sheriff and have him come see the sneaker and investigate the gully where it had been found.

About an hour later, the sheriff rushed up the driveway in his K10 Blazer, leaving a plume of dust in his wake. He and Deputy Davis knocked on the door, where Alice greeted them and welcomed them into the house. Nathan, fresh out of the shower, and the boys were waiting in the living room. They interrogated Jason and Tom about their story, and finding at least the part about where they found the shoe to be believable, went back out to the truck and radioed for backup, and a Kay-Nine unit if possible. Dispatch radioed back and said that the Sheriff's Department didn't have any available Kay-Nine's at the time, but that they could get some up from Anchorage by the evening.

"In the meantime," Callahan said to the boys after telling their mother the news on the hounds, "I think it's best if you take Deputy Davis and I on the same path that you took this morning."

Tom's face went white. "No, no, no, no, no!" He objected. "Sheriff, that monster's out there. He almost got us already, he'll get us for sure if we go back out."

Nathan placed his hand on his son's shoulder to calm him down. "It's okay, Tom," he said, "you'll have us with you this time. I'll have my rifle," he put heavy emphasis on the word 'I'.

"...And Davis and I will bring our shotguns along out of the truck." Callahan assured the frightened boy. "Nothing's gonna happen to you."

Jason sighed. "If you can guarantee our safety, we can show you I guess."

"Excellent," Callahan said.

"But what about mom?" Tom objected.

"What about me?" Asked Alice. "I'll be safe here, I promise."

Nathan gave her a kiss on the cheek. "My service revolver is in my desk-drawer in our bedroom if you need it, God forbid."

"I won't," Alice assured him, "but thank you."

The boys, Nathan, Callahan, and Deputy Davis set out up the driveway. The sun was out now and the thin layer of snow had completely melted. The chickadees had gone about their business, and the only sound was the crunching of feet on the gravel driveway. The troupe hooked a right at the mailbox, passed Harmony's empty grave, and marched near-silently to the North Gate.

"Look!" Tom said, picking up the plaster cast of the sasquatch print which was laying on top of the trail now that the snow had melted away. "The sasquatch left tracks! That's evidence!"

Sheriff Callahan nodded. "Let me have that," he said, producing a clear plastic zipper bag marked "EVIDENCE" from his coat-pocket. Tom wanted to object, but knew that this was now practically a criminal investigation and it was in his best interest to comply with the sheriff.

Begrudgingly, he handed over the cast. “Can I get it back when you’re done with it?” He asked, half-jokingly. “It’s possibly the most amazing track I’ve ever cast.”

“We’ll have to see,” said Callahan. He produced a disposable camera from another coat-pocket and took a picture of the log, then motioned at Deputy Davis, who placed a small red flag where the footprint had been. Callahan took another picture, then looked up and down the trail and said, “Well, boys, lead the way!”

Tom and Jason led the adults further down the trail, keeping an eye out for the sasquatch, but they didn’t hear anything in the woods. “I don’t hear anything,” Tom said.

“Me neither. Do you think he’s still here?” asked Jason.

Tom shrugged. “Maybe not. I popped him pretty good with the air-rifle. Maybe he ran off.”

“I certainly hope so,” Jason shuddered.

They made it to the eastern property line without incident and struck out south again down the fence-line towards the powerline trail, where they struck back out west. "This is about where we first encountered the creature," Tom said. Sheriff Callahan nodded and made a note in his notepad, then snapped more pictures with his disposable camera.

The band trekked back westward until they got to the ravine. Here, the boys got more somber. They led the adults down into the ravine and headed along it until they got to the spot where they had found the shoe. Again, the officers began taking pictures and sticking evidence flags in the ground. After walking the ravine for thirty feet up and down from the location where the boys had found the shoe, Sheriff Callahan took Tom's father aside.

"Nathan," Callahan said, "you might go ahead and take the boys and head back to the house. They might not want to be here when we find what I think we're going to find. You... might not want to be here if we find what we're going to find."

Nathan nodded, a look of sorrow on his face. He turned towards the slope leading out of the ravine. "Come on, boys," he said. Climbing up the ravine, he turned back at the law enforcement officers. "Hey, when I come back down, I'll bring a ladder. Make things easier."

---

Callahan laid out the extra arms he had brought onto the kitchen table. "We've got two carbines. I'll carry one, plus my sidearm. Someone else can carry the other. I've only got thirty rounds each for them, so do not miss. I've got this, a twelve-gauge shotgun, and twelve rounds of buckshot. Not sure that'll stop a sasquatch, but it'll definitely put a damper on his day. Finally, we've got this, the big boy." The old man produced a small green object the size and shape of a baseball from his pocket and set it gingerly on the table.

"Holy shit, Callahan!" Tom exclaimed. "Is that..."

"A grenade? Yup. Fragmentation grenade, the type that throws shit everywhere." Callahan answered Tom's unspoken question proudly.

"Are those even legal?" Elise asked, flustered.

Callahan laughed. "I'm ex military and law enforcement. Not much isn't legal for me. If we wanna kill a sasquatch though, it's gonna take more firepower than the average bear. Literally. Now, what's your plan?"

"Uh," Tom mumbled, "my plan was pretty much to call you."

Callahan gestured to himself. "Well, mission accomplished. We got any other guns? Explosives? Vehicles? What do you got for me?"

Tom gestured to the AR-15 by the door. "Got that. It's got twenty-six rounds, don't know if there's any more for it. And I've got my twenty-two pistol with another twenty-six rounds for it. Elise," he ordered his sister-in-law, "go check the closet in mom's room. See if dad's old rifle is still in there."

Elise nodded and crept into the master bedroom, coming back out with the rifle and two boxes of ammunition for it. "This should be plenty," she said. She set the rifle and ammunition on the table."

"Oh," Callahan said, "one more thing. I've been studying these guys for years now. I know how to track them."

"What, by their footprints?" Isabel asked.

Callahan shook his head. From his pocket he produced a small dart with some kind of computer chip inside a pill-looking canister in a little clear carrying case. "With this. It's a GPS tracker, a little more high-tech. I only have the one, so we'll have to be precise with it. Loads into the shotgun, fires like a slug. One chance to track the beast back to wherever he took Jason. That's all we've got."

---

The sasquatch shouting in the night seemed to have scared off the mountain lion, and Tom and his siblings didn't hear from her again. Unnerved by the creature's howl, they tried to distract themselves by "gambling" shots out of Jason's flask based on the outcome of checkers games. Elise was very good at checkers, and the others had all taken a swig twice before she even had her first sip from the flask.

"What the hell is that?" She asked, pulling a face as she swallowed the liquor.

Jason laughed, taking the flask from her and taking an unearned swig for himself. "It's hooch." He said.

"Hooch?" Tom asked.

"Moonshine. Applejack. Made it myself. Well, I didn't make the Georgia grain alcohol. I just infused it with the apple juice and cinnamon and shit. *I* think it's delicious."

"Delicious is one word for it," Elise groaned. "I think I'm good on having any more of that shit."

"Suit yourself," Jason said. He held the flask up for his baby brother. "Tom? You want some? Come on, toast to dad with me."

"That's not real applejack, you know," Tom lectured his brother. "*Real* applejack is made by fermenting apple juice, not by adding Everclear to it."

"Whatever, Mr. Know-It-All" Jason groaned. "Nobody likes a smartass. Just drink up. For dad."

Tom rolled his eyes and took the flask from his brother. He never could turn down a challenge from Jason. Tom looked the flask over and gave the golden liquid inside a tentative sniff, then raised it into the air and muttered "for dad" before taking a sip.

Elise laughed as Tom handed the flask back to Jason, but her face suddenly soured, transforming into a grotesque look of terror. Her lower lip trembled as if she were trying to speak but she couldn't get any words out.

"Elise?" Jason asked. "Are you okay? What is it?"

Slowly, Elise raised a single trembling finger. The other three followed her finger down her line-of-sight to the window above the kitchen sink across the room, where a dark copper-colored, hairy mass was staring into the cabin, watching them with beady, unblinking eyes. In the dim, flickering light coming from the fireplace, they could make out a broad, upturned ape-like nose, heavy brow ridge, and wide forehead sloping up to a crested scalp. The creature didn't appear to show any emotion. It just stood there, staring into the window, watching them, slowly shifting its weight from one foot to the other and back again.

Isabel unleashed a bloodcurdling scream, and the creature's face suddenly changed to a look of surprise. It raised its hackles and shrieked back to her, an unearthly grumbling bellow like a howler monkey. Its parted lips revealed a set of massive canines like a chimpanzee, each as big as a grown man's finger.

Pop! Pop! Pop! Pop! Pop! Pop!

Tom had regained his senses just enough to seize his brother's twenty-two handgun, and raised it to the window. Squeezing the trigger as rapidly as he could, he emptied the clip of all six shots. The gunshots, the sound of breaking glass, and the roar of the sasquatch as it cried out in pain deafened the siblings, and their own cries only added to the cacophony. The monster disappeared from the window just as suddenly as it appeared, and through the haze that the gun had released into the cabin Tom could see why - the shattered glass that now covered the kitchen sink and counters was speckled with dark crimson blood. The beast had been hit.

"Did you kill it?" Jason shouted over the ringing of his own ears.

"I don't think so," Tom replied, gesturing to the window where the grouping of his shots was evidently not very tight. "I think I only hit it once. Maybe grazed it with another. If anything, I've just pissed it off." He released the clip from the handgun and held it out to his brother. "Hand me another six rounds."

Jason shook his head. "Tom, that's all that I brought with me."

Isabel's voice trembled, like she was on the verge of tears. "You mean we're defenseless?"

"If it comes back, yeah." Tom replied, setting the handgun down on the mantle.

"Well then," Jason shuddered, "we better pray like hell that it doesn't come back."

## Chapter Thirteen

At around three or four in the morning, the Carlinis decided it was best to at least try to get some sleep. None of them would, of course. Who would be able to sleep after seeing that grotesque head peeking through the window? Elise kept thinking back to the horror that she had felt, as she now lay with her face to the wall in an effort to not even have to glimpse at the single window in the cabin bedroom lest the creature stare back at her. Tom had taken the checkerboard and fixed it in place over the window with duct tape to keep the bugs from getting in at least, but it felt like the safety and integrity of the little cabin had been violated. So, the four Carlinis lay in their bunks sleeplessly, hoping that the beast wouldn't return.

By three in the morning, the earliest rays of the dawn's light had started to brighten the forest just the slightest bit. Tom, not being able to sleep, decided to leave his bunk and go back out into the main room of the cabin. Jason, still laying sleeplessly as well, heard Tom leave and elected to follow him.

Out in the main room, Jason asked Tom in a hushed whisper, "Do you think it's safe for us to stay here any longer?"

"Without ammunition? No. Do you have more at the house?"

"Yeah," Jason said, "I brought a full box so I should have twenty-four more rounds in my Jeep."

"We should've taken the Jeep here last night," Tom groaned. "Walking was foolish, not to mention dangerous."

Jason nodded in agreement. "No use beating ourselves up over the past. Do you think the sasquatch is between us and the house?"

"Honestly?" Tom replied, "there's no way to know, but our safest bet is going to be to assume the worst. Do you remember how it followed us when we were boys, Jason? How it *hunted* us?"

Jason shivered in the chilly morning air, but didn't respond to his brother. Instead, he took the fireplace poker and stirred the embers of last night's fire to get it going again. "Get me two more logs," he instructed his brother.

Tom fetched two more logs from the wood-cart, being careful again to not grab any spiders, and passed them to his brother, who put them in the fireplace. “Jason, I think we’re in serious danger as long as we stay here. Not just us, but Isabel, and Elise, and mom, too.”

“Mom’s at the house,” Jason assured his brother. “She’s safe.”

“Is she?” Tom prodded. “Jason, he tried to get in here. What’s to stop him from getting in there?”

Jason paused. “Mom has dad’s hunting rifle.”

“Yeah, but does she know how to use it?”

“She knows how to use it.”

“Come on, Jace. We can’t stay here. We gotta get back to the house. We gotta wake mom up and get all of us out of here. It’s just not safe to stay here with that monster around. Not just here, but the house too. The whole property. None of it is safe. It’s. Not. Safe. Here.”

Jason dropped the fire-poker and turned quickly, closing the distance between him and his brother in two quick strides. He drew close to Tom’s face, looking him dead in the eye. “Listen to me, Tom. This is our home. Not his. Ours.

We're not letting him run us off. We've lost too much already to the woods. Dad, Harmony, we're not losing paradise too." His eyes darted between Tom's, then he took a deep breath and backed off a little bit. "I'm sorry, Tom, I didn't mean to get in your face. This property, it just means a lot to me, that's all. It… it means everything to me. This is home."

Tom nodded. "Alright, Jason." Jason turned and continued tending to the fire.

"What's going on?" Elise asked, standing in the doorway to the bedroom. She had been awake the entire time, and had been brought out to the living room by the sound of voices. "Are you two okay?"

"It's nothing, Elise," Jason assured her. "Go back to bed."

"I can't sleep," she said. "That… thing. That thing freaked me out too bad."

"Is Isabel awake?" Tom asked.

"I think so. I don't think she feels safe in this cabin either," Elise said. "I think we'd both feel safer in the actual house, not this decrepit shit-shack."

Tom tried his hardest to not appear like he was bragging as he turned to his brother. “Well that settles it then, doesn't it?” He asked. “Let's head back to the house.”

Jason shook his head. “Not before it's light. If anything, I'll head back, get the Jeep, and come pick the rest of you up.”

“Alone?” Elise asked.

“Of course not,” Jason answered. “Tom's coming with me.”

---

There was a knock on the door. Alice and Nathan Carlini answered together to find Sheriff Callahan standing somberly with his hat in his hands. Deputy Davis was behind him with another deputy they hadn't met before, both looking at the ground and also holding their hats in their hands.

“Yes?” Alice asked. “What is it, Sheriff?”

“Alice and Nathan Carlini, may I come in? You may want to sit down for this.”

Alice beckoned the three men in. “Of course. Come, sit down.”

Andrew Callahan waited for the couple to sit, then spoke. This was always his least favorite part of the job, breaking bad news to the next of kin. "Mrs. Carlini," he said, "I'm so sorry, but the cadaver dogs found your daughter in the ravine."

Both Alice and Nathan broke when Andrew Callahan spoke those words, but in different ways. Alice had a very physical breakdown. She dropped to her knees and screamed and cried, the sort of wail that is only made by a mother who has lost her child. Nathan kept a brave face for his wife at the time, but later that night in private behind closed doors, once Alice and the boys had gone to bed, he would break down alone in the shower and cry.

Harmony Carlini was pronounced dead as soon as her body made it to the morgue. Her cause of death was ruled to be blunt force injuries sustained by a wild animal, and was never investigated further in any official capacity. She hadn't even quite made it a mile from the driveway where she had last been seen. Her death had likely come mere minutes after she left Nathan's sight, though her body had likely been moved around before eventually being deposited in the ravine and buried by that year's spring rains.

After his daughter was officially ruled dead, Nathan Carlini buried himself in his work. When he wasn't working, he was drinking. He remained a shell of his former self until his untimely death nearly a decade later in 2001. Around the time of Nathan's death, Alice's mind began to slip. The doctors called it early onset dementia, but Jason and Tom knew that what it really meant was that they were losing their mother too. To Tom, it seemed like his sister, his sweet, brightly smiling sister who could light up any room she walked into, was the glue that held the Carlini family together. They truly would never recover from her loss.

Andrew Callahan, in the meantime, continued to investigate the death of Harmony Carlini. How did a little girl disappear for several months, avoid a search party of nearly one hundred people, and then show back up in a frequently traveled ravine less than a mile away from where she had disappeared from? His work investigating the girl's disappearance wasn't supported by the Sheriff's Department. In fact, he was told multiple times to drop the case. It likely was a contributing factor to his unexpected retirement six years later in 1998.

When the story broke that the Harmony Carlini case had been solved and a body had been found, it made its rounds in the national media again. The Carlinis got lots of letters and gift-baskets and even visitors, so many even that the Sheriff's Department had to station a patrol-car outside of their home for several weeks until the unwanted visitors stopped making their way out. It being the early days of the internet, the very first internet sleuths also took up the case."What could have happened to Harmony Carlini," they speculated - often overlooking the devastating reality that this mystery involved a real child's death and a family's unbearable loss. Some even said that Nathan had to have been the killer, since he was the last person who saw her alive. Obviously, this only had a negative effect on the Carlini patriarch's mental state.

In many ways, the disappearance of Harmony Carlini became the sole event that the history of the entire Carlini family hinged on. Whereas other tragedies bring people together, though, Harmony's death and later Nathan's only tore the family apart. The boys moved down to the Lower Forty-Eight, to Missouri and Texas, and started their own families. After Nathan died, Alice would eventually leave the property as well. Harmony and her father lay buried in the forest of the Alaskan Mountains, the sole remnants of the homestead that was once so full of life.

The house and hunting cabin sat empty in the woods. The Carlini paradise was no more.

---

Tom definitely had second thoughts about leaving the girls alone and defenseless in the cabin, but once he and Jason left them locked up tight and wandered out into the open, dimly lit forest, his reservations started to fade. A cool wind blew steadily off the mountains to the east, and a thick fog blanketed the forest. The little light that came in from the impending sunrise refracted everywhere, giving the woods an eerie effervescent glow. Tom and Jason stuck together within arms reach of each other, and treaded carefully on the gravel trail, to minimize the amount of noise they made. They listened carefully for the monster, expecting it to be lurking somewhere in the shadowy forest, but besides their own breath and footsteps they didn't hear a sound.

By the time they made it back to the house, the wind had picked up a little bit. The fog was growing into a dense haze, and the light of the sunrise was fading again. Thunderstorms weren't uncommon this time of the year, especially early in the morning, but heavy rain could quickly make the road back to the cabin all but unpassable, particularly where it crossed the ravine which would flood and quickly swell into a raging river with the stormwater. Jason sent Tom into the house to check on Alice while he went to put the roof up on his Jeep and prepare it for the rainy journey.

Tom reentered the house through the back door, being careful to open and shut it as quietly as he could. He crept into his mother's bedroom where she was asleep alone on her marital bed and checked the closet, where he was incredibly grateful to find his father's old bolt-action rifle still resting. He grabbed it and a box of cartridges, then went back out front to meet Jason.

Tom threw the rifle across the backseat of the Jeep and helped his brother secure the brown vinyl ragtop in place. He then climbed into the passenger seat and his brother started the Jeep. As it began to rain, they raced down the trail back towards the hunting cabin.

Back at the cabin, the girls had further barricaded the broken window and door using the furniture, and were waiting for Jason and Tom to return. They were greatly disturbed by the silence outside, and sat in their own silence in the living room, hardly daring to breathe for fear of the creature returning. Isabel had known of the existence of the beast, because Tom had told her plenty and she believed him, but Elise never actually believed in sasquatch until she saw him with her very own eyes just a few hours ago. Now, they sat criss-cross on the floor in front of the fire, the fireplace poker - which was the single best potential weapon in the house - resting between them.

There was a banging noise outside that made both girls jump. “What was that?” Isabel asked, her voice trembling.

"I think... I think it's throwing rocks at the cabin." Elise said. "Do they do that?"

Another crashing sound deafened the two. This time, the rock clattered onto the cabin's tin roof, making Isabel cry out. "What are we going to do?"

Elise clutched the fireplace poker. "Not much we can do," she said. "Tom emptied the twenty-two. Just hope they're back soon with more firepower."

Another rock thudded against the side of the house, and then another, and then the barrage seemed to stop. Elise loosened her grip on the poker. "Is... Is it gone?" She asked tentatively.

The sasquatch seemed to respond from outside with a haunting yell, followed seconds later by a howling call. It was so loud, it rattled the remaining windows of the little cabin. Elise yelled "Go away!" And the sasquatch barked back at her.

The creature climbed up to the cabin's front porch, the wooden boards creaking under its immense weight, and pounded twice on the door. The girls could hear it sniffing around, its fingers running around the door trying to figure it out. It took the door-handle and shook the door three times, but the deadbolt held. Elise took up the poker and stood up, charging at the door yelling at the top of her lungs. She slammed the blunt end of the poker into the door twice, making as much noise as she possibly could.

The sasquatch roared on the front porch and punched the door in frustration, the sound of its fist on wood making her jump again. She then heard it turn and step off of the porch. Elise rested her back against the wall beside the door and breathed a sigh of relief.

There was a crashing noise, and the sound of broken glass. Across from the window that had been knocked out with a rock, the sasquatch's arm reached into the cabin through another newly broken window and groped around on the wall in the direction of Elise. The beast was so close, she could make out the reddish hairs erupting from the black skin of the hand, which was the size of a dinner plate. Each curling black finger ended in long, gnarled fingernails like talons. Elise froze, terrified, not even able to breathe as the massive hand reached in her direction.

Without even knowing what she was doing, Isabel rose to her feet and let out a terrifying war-cry. She charged across the cabin, picking up a ladder-back chair as she ran. The sasquatch stopped groping around the wall as it tried to evaluate the situation, and Isabel placed the chair in front of her body and crashed into the wall with her entire weight, smashing the beast's arm between the chair and the wall. The sasquatch bellowed in pain, and Isabel could feel its immense strength as it threw her off the wall and drew its arm back out the window.

As the hand retreated, it gripped the side of the window momentarily, but cut itself on a jagged piece of glass sticking out from the window-frame. Thinking quickly, Isabel snatched the piece of glass free from the adhesive that held it. Wielding it like a dagger, she raised her fist and then plunged the glass into the creature's hand.

The creature roared with pain, and Isabel beamed with accomplishment. "Look out!" Elise cried, and she started to raise her hand back up just as the sasquatch's other hand reached into the window and grabbed her arm with vice-like strength. Isabel felt the bones in her forearm moving in a way they shouldn't, and as the sasquatch yanked she wondered if her shoulder would give first or if the beast would drag her back out through the window. She screamed in a combination of fury and terror and dropped the glass. Elise, now spurred out of her paralysis, crossed the room, picked up the poker, and with a shout mustered all of her strength and smacked the beast's hand with it.

The beast didn't even flinch, and continued to squeeze down on Isabel's arm. "The fire, Elise!" Isabel yelled, pointing with her other hand towards the still-lit fireplace. Elise crossed the room again and reached into the fireplace. The adrenaline coursing through her veins kept her from even feeling the heat at first as she grabbed one of the flaming logs out of the hearth and ran back across the room with it. Yelling with rage and pain, she swung the burning branch and struck the sasquatch's hand with it. The sasquatch roared and released Isabel, who collapsed to the floor out of its reach. It retracted its hand from the window, and Elise stuck her upper half out the broken pane. She spotted the beast, falling backwards onto its posterior on the ground below and clutching its injured arm. With a haunting scream, she threw the burning log out the window, striking the sasquatch in the chest with it. The creature roared with fear and scrambled to stand up, where it turned to run.

Boom! Boom! Boom! Boom! The sound of Nathan's hunting rifle was much deeper, and much more menacing, than the twenty-two had been. Elise flinched and covered her face with her blistered and burnt hand as three of the bullets exploded against the porch and wall around her. The fourth bullet grazed the sasquatch, and it roared one more time. Scrambling and stumbling over its own big feet, it clambered off into the forest.

Elise drew back into the window, clutching her hand which she could now tell had been badly burned. She sank to the floor and began to sob beside Isabel, who was nursing her arm. Already the bruises were beginning to show deep purple where the sasquatch had grabbed her, and her fingers felt cold, stiff, and unmoving. Blood soaked her arm from the multiple lacerations the shattered windowpane had inflicted. Suddenly there was a pounding on the door. Both girls shrieked.

"Open up!" Jason's voice came from outside. "We've got the Jeep and the rifle, and we're going to get you out of here!"

## Chapter Fourteen

"What do you mean you've been studying sasquatches?" Elise asked.

Andrew Callahan nodded towards Tom. "His sister disappeared in these woods in 1992. I was the sheriff at the time, and was the officer who responded. When we found her, the official cause of death came back as 'blunt force trauma likely caused by a wild animal.' But we're in Alaska. What kind of a wild animal would be causing blunt force trauma here? A bear? No, it had to be something else.

"So I started asking around. Parks and Wildlife, NPS, BLM, anyone I could think of who had relevant experience and law enforcement ties. They all came up just as blank as I was. That's when I started posting on the internet. Tons of people were already discussing the case online, it was huge even for those early days of the internet. People are obsessed with mystery. I was able to blend into the crowd online without raising too much suspicion, and that's where I first came across the sasquatch theory.

"Then I delved into research on the sasquatch legend. It turns out, there's a fairly large network of people who've been studying them, regarding them as real creatures, more or less in secret to avoid ridicule by the larger scientific community. Cryptozoologists, they call themselves. They'll study the Loch Ness Monster, shadow people, dinosaurs and pterosaurs that are supposed to have survived into the twentieth century, and my personal favorite, those little wiggly things that you sometimes see in pictures that people say are bugs. Rods, they call them. Supposedly invisible creatures that live in the sky and are responsible for missing persons cases.

"But it kept coming back to the sasquatch legend. Turns out, these creatures live on three continents. Used to be four, but they got wiped out from Europe it seems. But they're super common. Most of 'em are peaceful, hiding out in the woods and in the mountains and only coming out to look for something to eat. Read about a hundred sasquatch encounters and ninety-nine of them will be 'I saw it off in the trees' or 'it was snoopin' around my property'. Almost never do any real damage. But then there were three other cases I found where that wasn't the case.

"First off, back in the 1800s, the settlers and lumberjacks who first moved into this area reported strange monkey-like beasts with no tails that lived up in the trees and threw stuff at them while they tried to work. Called them acropelters."

"The sasquatch certainly likes throwing things," Tom said.

"Precisely. It's now thought that acropelters were just baby apes defending their territory from what they considered a safe vantage point. In 1924, a man named Albert something-or-other claimed to have been carried off by a sasquatch and kept as a pet for over a week. But then here's where it really gets creepy.

"In this very stretch of woods in 1964, a man by the name of James Jonas was pulled from his truck and mutilated in an apparent wild animal attack. The same week, photographs of a sasquatch were taken. Here." He reached into his coat-pocket and pulled out two prints of a photograph, which he handed to Tom.

"Ho-lee-shit," Tom said, "that's our ape. I'd recognize his ugly mug anywhere."

"Thought he might be. Same ape, sighted outside Susitna in '84. Stole fruit left to dry in a barn and carried off the family dog. Wasilla, '88, same sasquatch was photographed stalking a couple of teenagers pulled over at Makeout Point. '90, your neighbors the Molinas reported that rock-throwing incident. I knew what was up."

"And then Harmony in '92," Elise mused.

"Exactly!" Callahan cawed. "Makes too much sense to be a coincidence, right? It's a pattern. It all makes sense when you take a step back and look at it with an open mind."

"So this ape," Tom said, "he's been killing in the area for what? Fifty years?"

"More like sixty," Callahan corrected him, "if you start with James Jonas. That's if you assume they were all the same ape, and I do. I've encountered a sasquatch or two in my studies, and most of them are harmless, shy even. They want nothing to do with people. Not the Mat-Su Ape. He's sadistic and cruel and for some reason really loves abducting people and carrying them off into the forest still screaming."

"Then it's settled," Tom stood up. "We need to put a stop to him once and for all."

"Where do we start?" Isabel asked.

Callahan turned to her, glimpsing at the sleeping children in the next room. "Can you drive a manual?"

"Y… yes," she said.

He tossed her the keys to his Blazer. "Get the kids. Get Alice. Get them all in the truck. We'll provide security while you load up. Take them into town, take them to the Calvary Christian Church. That's probably the safest place for them that'll still be open at this hour. Take the twenty-two for protection. It's better than nothing. Get them to safety, then head back this way."

She took the keys and nodded, then went to the living room to rouse the children. Tom and Elise each took a carbine rifle to escort everyone out to the truck. Tom went back into the master bedroom and gently shook Alice and Samuel awake. "Mom, we gotta go," he said. "It's not safe here."

"What's going on?" she asked. "Why isn't it safe here?"

"There's a monster here who wants to hurt us," he said. He didn't have time to explain further. He helped his mother get dressed and led her out to Isabel.

"Wait," said Samuel. "Let me take her. It's my job to take care of her."

Isabel paused, not wanting to leave her mother, but conceded. Samuel had plenty of fight in him, and he had taken care of her mother so far. She would let him do this for her. She sighed and handed him the keys.

With the carbines, he and Elise escorted the children out to the truck and helped them buckle in where they could along the two bench seats. Tom looked Samuel dead in the eyes. "Don't stop until you make it to town. Assume the woods are not safe. Shoot first and ask questions later. Keep the doors locked. Drive carefully. We know his tricks, he likes to jump out in front of cars and make them crash. Don't fall for it. Come right back here after."

"I'll get them there safe," Samuel promised. He shut the truck door and engaged the locks, then started the engine. Tom waved goodbye to them as he turned around and rumbled down the driveway.

Back inside the house, Tom, Callahan, Isabel, and Elise gathered to devise a plan to kill the sasquatch and rescue Jason. "We just need to lure it here and then fill it full of lead and kill it, right?" Elise asked, gesturing towards the table full of guns.

"The first thing we need," Callahan said, shaking his head, "is to find out where it's taken Jason. That miner I was telling you about, Albert Ostman? He said that when he was abducted, the sasquatch took him back to its home in a cave and held him captive for six days. If our sasquatch did the same thing to Jason, there's a very good chance that we can trick it into leading us right to him." He picked up the GPS device off the table. "That's where this bad boy comes in.

"What we do is we lay a trap. We bait the sasquatch into getting into close range, then shoot it with the tracker. From there, it's just a matter of following it back, taking it out, and, lord willing, rescuing Jason."

Tom scratched his head. "How do we bait a sasquatch?"

As the Blazer hurried down the road into town, Samuel remembered the warning he had been issued. "It likes to jump out in front of you," he mused to himself, trying to keep his eyes peeled as best as he could. Behind him, the kids whined in the back seat, and Alice joined in their lament. "Quiet," he said calmly. "We're going to be alright. We'll get somewhere safe and go back to sleep."

The truck rounded a corner and Samuel slowed. The road ahead got tight, and it was dark in the woods. He didn't like it at all. He slowed to a near crawl and kept his eyes peeled.

With a bang, a rock hit the hood of the truck. The children screamed in horror. The monster had found them. With no choice, Samuel hit the gas. The wheels spun in the gravel, and the truck lurched forward, bouncing down the rutted old road urgently. He rounded a corner and the left two wheels almost left the ground, and then...

The creature stepped out into the road in front of him. He overcorrected and almost swerved into a tree. Everyone in the vehicle screamed, including him as the truck spun out, coming to rest sideways in the road with the monster to his left. It reared itself up to its full height and roared.

Samuel didn't know what else to do. He roared back.

The creature was startled. It hadn't expected that. It backed off a step or two, and Samuel saw his chance. He swung the door open and scooped a rock off the ground. Roaring again, he threw the rock as hard as he could.

It connected with the sasquatch right on top of its head. The creature let out a startled grunt, turned tail, and ran off into the forest.

## Chapter Fifteen

The sasquatch hunters slept in shifts that night, and at about five in the morning, Andrew Callahan roused them all from their slumber to enact his plan. They got dressed in the most protective clothes they had available, double-checked all their weapons, then wrapped themselves in blankets where they could easily conceal their rifles. They rubbed alcohol on their lips and applied extra deodorant, to be as smelly as possible without actually letting themselves be intoxicated, then they opened the sliding glass door at the back of the house and filed out into the pre-dawn forest.

Walking down the trail to the hunting cabin, they laughed wildly, hooted, hollered, and sang. They had no neighbors for a mile around to worry about, and wanted to attract the attention of the one other soul out in the woods that night. They flashed their flashlights up into the trees and even higher into the low clouds overhead, letting out a beacon to broadcast their location.

When they got to the cabin, the party only grew. They lit a brilliant fire in the hearth, and another one in the fire-pit outside. Callahan produced an old guitar from the recesses of the cabin, and they sat around on the porch playing music loudly and poorly singing along. Tom had brought with him a flask of cheap whiskey, which he liberally poured onto the ground to create as much of a stink as possible.

Between verses of a camp-song Callahan had taught them about an ant and a rubber-tree, Tom looked at Callahan and touched his nose. He was silently communicating that he had noticed a skunky, foul smell on the air. Callahan sniffed, and nodded, turning to the others and gesturing to his nose to convey the message to Isabel and Elise. The skunk-ape, as they were aptly called throughout the south, neared.

Tom stood up and loudly announced, “I’m tired, and the sun’s nearly up! I think it's time for me to hit the hay! Isabel, are you coming?”

“Yes,” Isabel answered, just as loudly, “I’m right behind you, babe.” The two stood up, hugged Elise goodnight, and went inside, letting the cabin door slam behind them.

“Well,” Elise turned to Callahan, “looks like it’s just you and me, old man.”

"Yes," Callahan said, "I'm going to get another drink. Would you like one?"

"Why, yes please!" Elise exclaimed. "I'll just wait out here alone on the porch!"

Callahan nodded, letting his eye contact linger with Elise for a moment, then rose to his feet and went inside, overexaggerating his footsteps on the porch and letting the door slam behind him.

Elise was now alone on the porch, where eighteen years prior she and her sister-in-law had been attacked by the creature. Her blood ran cold, suddenly realizing how terribly horribly wrong this plan could potentially go. Was she crazy to have agreed to it? She had the twenty-two tucked under her blanket in case things went south, but she seriously doubted the miniscule handgun's stopping power against a six-hundred pound raging sasquatch. The smell had intensified, and she heard a low whistling noise out in the woods. A twig snapped, startling an owl, and she suddenly felt the feeling that she was being watched. Now, she had to act like everything was okay. She started to hum to herself and feigned a drunken smile.

Inside the house, Tom and Isabel were ducked down behind the front window with their carbine rifles ready, in case the plan went south. Callahan had the shotgun, which he had loaded with the tracking chip. He was pressed up against the front door waiting for his cue, ready to spring out and tag the beast. “God, please let this work,” he whispered a prayer out. If they failed to tag the beast, they might never see Jason or Elise alive ever again.

A low whistling sound floated out of the forest. It definitely didn’t sound like a bird to Elise. It sounded exactly like a human whistling a single low note, but there was definitely something… off about it. It made Elise’s skin crawl. *Please, Callahan, please know what you’re doing,* she thought.

She herself started whistling the tune to the song they had been singing minutes before. He’s got high hopes, he’s got try hopes. He’s got cherry pie in July hopes…

In the flickering light of the campfire in the yard below her, she could make out movement at the treeline. She didn’t dare look directly at the sasquatch, wanting it to believe that it was taking her off guard, but her memories went back again to when it had previously attacked them in 2002. It was definitely the same sasquatch. It *smelled* exactly the same. She would never forget that smell.

Oops, there goes another rubber tree plant.

A terrifying, roaring yell erupted from the treeline, splitting the otherwise silent night like a chisel. Elise didn't even have time to react - the sasquatch had dropped to all fours and was now barreling down on her. At a speed of nearly forty miles an hour, it closed the distance to the porch effortlessly and was on top of her. Elise tried to scream, but found she was absolutely paralyzed by fear. The beast grabbed her in its massive hands, vice-like grip holding her to the point where she felt like she would break. *This is it,* she thought. *This is how I die.* The mental image of the trucker found ripped apart from Callahan's story came floating into her mind. The sasquatch sniffed her, and she closed her eyes and braced for the worst.

The front door of the cabin opened. "Hey, you ugly fucker!" Callahan shouted.

Surprised, the sasquatch dropped Elise, and she fell limply to the cabin porch by his feet. The sasquatch turned to face Callahan, confused. It reared up to its full height and roared at him. Elise could see Tom and Isabel in the window getting ready to open fire, and crossed her fingers hoping the plan would work.

"Eat lead." Callahan pulled the shotgun's trigger.

The blast of the shotgun inches from Elise's face was deafening. She heard a roar, and then nothing but a ringing sound, but what she felt was pain. White hot, searing pain ripped through her body, but it seemed most concentrated on her face. Dropping to the fetal position and letting out a scream, she felt the sensation of liquid trickling from her ear - the remains of her shattered eardrum, no doubt. But when she went to wipe it off she was taken off-guard by what felt like stringy bits of raw bacon hanging from the side of her head. She took one between her fingers and pulled and it fell away. Clutching it in her hand, she brought herself to peek at it between her fingers.

It was all that was left of her ear.

Above her, the sasquatch roared with anger as the tracking chip struck it directly in the chest and embedded itself into its skin. It lunged at Callahan, trying to snatch the shotgun out of his hand, but he had already rolled back and slammed the door shut, falling backwards onto his ass into the cabin. "Now!" He shouted.

Tom and Isabel pivoted into the open doorway and opened fire with the carbines, popping off four shots each in rapid succession. They weren't necessarily aiming for the sasquatch and didn't care if they hit it. The whizzing of bullets past it was more than enough to scare it into retreating. It bellowed in anger, dropped off the porch, and barreled off into the forest on all fours, crying out in the distance as it disappeared into the early morning.

Isabel cried out and ran onto the porch to help her sister-in-law up. She said words, but Elise couldn't hear them over the ringing in her ears. "Oh god!" Elise exclaimed. "I can't hear anything! I think I've gone deaf!"

"It's okay," Isabel tried to console her. She moved Elise's face to where her eyes could read her lips and spoke very slowly. "I'm sure it's temporary. You'll be fine. Let's get you inside." Pulling off her hoodie, she clumped it into a makeshift bandage and pressed it against the remains of her sister-in-law's ear. "Hold this here," she ordered.

"Did it work?" Tom asked Callahan, eagerly.

Callahan produced a satellite phone from his pocket. He entered the cabin, closing and latching the door behind him, and booted up the phone. "Someone cover up that window," he ordered, gesturing towards the front window that had been ripped apart with gunfire. He fiddled with the phone, and a map of the surrounding forest appeared on the screen. A white dot centered around the cabin, with a red blip on it moving rapidly away from it. "Ladies and gentlemen," Callahan grinned, "we've got him!"

Tom hurried over to Callahan and looked at the dot on the screen, letting out a whoop of mixed joy and relief. "Come on, baby," he said, "take us to Jason."

Elise held her hand up to her ear to try and stop the pain, and it came away wetted with crimson blood. "Uh, guys?" She managed to say before the sight of her own blood made her eyes roll back into her head as she collapsed.

Fortunately for Elise, Callahan knew how to react in an emergency situation. He ripped off the blanket he was still wearing, which he had used to conceal the shotgun, and pressed it to Elise's head to still the bleeding. "She needs a hospital," he said. "Tom, Isabel, run back to the house and get my truck. I'll call nine-one-one."

Tom nodded. "Come on, Isabel." They took a second to reload their rifles before heading out into the foggy woods, then disappeared northwards towards the house.

Callahan pressed the blanket to Elise's head, then took her hand and pressed it into it to convey the message to her. "You've got to keep pressure on it," he said loudly and slowly, hoping that she could read his lips. "You don't want to bleed out through your ear. Your hearing will return, but the blood-loss is a serious threat."

Elise nodded, and laid down on the couch with her bloodied ear facing up. She pressed the blanket to it and shut her eyes and waited. Callahan dialed nine-one-one.

"Emergency services," the lady on the phone said, "how can I assist?"

"This is former sheriff Andrew Callahan," he replied coolly and calmly. "I need EMS to coordinates six-two point three-six-oh-five, neg-one-four-nine point three-oh-two-three. Hurry. I have a victim of firearm-related ear damage, bleeding from her ear. You'll need a helicopter, the roads are bad."

"Yes sir," the dispatcher replied. "Stay calm, keep compression on that to prevent bleeding. We have a medevac unit deploying out of Anchorage, ETA forty minutes."

---

This time as Tom and Isabel hurried back to the house, they kept their voices down and their flashlights aimed at the ground. Still carrying their carbine rifles, they practically ran the entire way. They had left the AR-15 with Callahan to defend Elise if necessary, but Tom secretly and selfishly wished that he had taken it for himself. It was about a mile back to the house, and the pair made it in ten minutes' time.

Once again rounding the front of the house to where Samuel had just parked the Blazer, Isabel climbed into the driver seat as Tom hopped into the right side and the doctor climbed into the back. Isabel cranked the engine and threw the truck into gear and tore off down the gravel driveway around the house and back towards the cabin. The truck was much noisier than they had been on foot, and Isabel watched the rear view mirror nervously for the sasquatch behind them. Even in a motor vehicle, she wasn't sure that she could outrun it on the bumpy, rutted out road, especially in the ancient Blazer which showed all its nearly forty years of age and creaked and twisted at the frame as she hurried down the road.

As Isabel arrived at the cabin, Tom undid his seatbelt. He jumped out of the truck before she even had it in park and ran back up to the porch, where he pounded on the front door. "Callahan!" He called. "It's Tom! I've got the truck!"

The old man swung the door open, rifle in his hand just in case. Tom realized how grizzled and disheveled the former sheriff looked, and it occurred to him that he probably looked similar himself. Bags had formed under Callahan's eyes, and he was spattered with dried blood - both Elise's and the sasquatch's. He motioned for Tom to come in, and Isabel followed closely behind, still clutching her carbine as well.

"How is she?" Samuel asked, as he entered the cabin.

Callahan grimaced. "Not great. She's lost a lot of blood, and is getting delirious."

The doctor grimaced and started tending to her wounds. "I can't fix her here," he said, "but I can keep her safe until help arrives."

Tom locked the front door and set the carbine down under the broken window. "As long as she's alive, that's what matters. What about the bigfoot?"

Callahan suddenly realized that he hadn't checked the tracker in nearly twenty minutes, having minimized it to use his satellite-phone to call nine-one-one. He tabbed back over to the tracker app and watched it for a minute while Isabel and Tom tended to Elise. "Well I'll be," he said after watching for a minute.

"What is it?" The other three all said together.

Callahan held out the phone for the others to see. "The tracker's stopped on the property. In the ravine, half a mile from where they found your sister."

---

Callahan and Tom sat out on the front porch waiting for the medevac chopper, while Isabel tended to her sister-in-law. Tom was musing over the rest of the plan, thinking about everything that could possibly go wrong. It was growing light now, and he liked the idea of facing the beast in daylight a lot more than it coming to them at night. Still, it wasn't a perfect plan.

"What if the tracker just fell out of its chest?" Tom asked Callahan.

"Well," Callahan responded, "then we just have to hope that the sumbitch is dumb enough to fall for our tricks again."

"And what if he doesn't have Jason?"

"Then we call in a standard search-and-rescue, advised that there may be a dangerous animal on the loose."

"And what if we don't recover him then?"

Callahan looked Tom up and down. "Oh, we'll recover him then, son. Don't you worry. I'll see to that. When I was elected to the position of Sheriff more than thirty years ago, I swore an oath to protect and serve the people who live here. I intend to keep my word. And Tom? I swore an oath to your dad too. When he died. I swore to protect you and your brother and your mom. And I intend to keep my word there too. For your dad. He saved my life. It's the least I can do."

There was a rumbling sound in the distance. Tom thought it was thunder at first, but then he realized that it was a helicopter. He stuck his head in the cabin door and called for Isa. "Hey, babe! The helicopter's almost here! Need help prepping her for transport?"

"We could use it, yeah." Isabel responded. "She's still lucid, but just barely."

Tom looked back out at Callahan. "I'm gonna help prep her," he said.

Callahan smiled. "Family caring for family. Love to see it. Just wait until I get your brother back." He stepped off the porch to wave the helicopter down.

Tom smiled and stepped into the house. "Come on, I'll help carry her out." He, Samuel, and Isabel picked up Elise, and together they carried her out into the yard. The helicopter touched down next to the smoldering fire-pit and two paramedics jumped out. They helped Tom load her up, assured him that she would be fine and that, in the worst case scenario, she'd lose hearing in the one ear, and the helicopter took off towards the sky, bearing Tom's sister skyward. Samuel rode with for his own conscience. They watched the helicopter disappear over the horizon, heading south towards Anchorage.

Once the helicopter vanished, Callahan turned to the others and clapped his hands. “Welp,” he sucked air between his teeth. “We’ve got work to do. Let’s get this sumbitch and save your brother!”

The three gathered their weapons and piled into Callahan’s Blazer, the former sheriff back at the wheel of his own truck, and they headed back north to the farmhouse. Tom held Callahan’s satellite phone, and watched the GPS dot that represented the sasquatch to make sure that it didn’t respond to the noise from the helicopter or the truck. Isabel, riding shotgun, wielded the AR-15.

They drove back up to the house, amazed at how much the forest was coming alive in the morning air. As the fog rolled off the mountains, they even caught a good amount of sun filtering through the smokey air above them. Callahan breathed deeply and sighed, “God I love these mountains.”

Parking in front of the house, they disembarked from the Blazer and re-entered the house. Tom handed the satellite phone back to Callahan. “It hasn’t moved,” he reported. “If I had to guess, it’s retired for the day. Hopefully with my brother.”

Callahan took the phone. “Perfect. I didn’t want to have to track a moving target. Help me gather every gun we have and load them into the Blazer.” He paused for a second and picked the fragmentation grenade up off the kitchen table. “And this little guy. I’ll hold onto him.”

Tom and Isabel swept the house to make sure they had gotten all the guns. In the daylight, they were able to better check out the wreckage of Jason’s pickup truck as well, and they found an extra three-eighty revolver tucked handily into the glovebox. “I’m sure Jason will want to be reunited with this,” Callahan said as he gingerly placed it in the backseat of the Blazer. Climbing into the front seat, he called to the others, “Last chance! Go now if you need to! I’m not pulling over once we leave!”

## Chapter Sixteen

It had been thirty minutes since the sasquatch had moved. Callahan hoped that meant that it was sleeping. It would be a much-needed stroke of good luck to catch the creature off-guard. The plan was simple - travel to the dot on the map, locate the sasquatch, locate Jason, subdue the sasquatch by any means necessary, liberate Jason. *Plans are always simple on paper,* thought Tom.

Callahan drove the Blazer down to the old wooden bridge where the trail crossed the gully and parked the Blazer just past the ravine. Still watching the GPS tracker, Tom took his brother's AR-15. Callahan took his shotgun and strapped it to his back, ensured that his nine-millimeter sidearm was still on his hip, then took one of the carbine rifles. Elise took the twenty-two and placed it on her hip, then seized the other carbine. There was no need for blankets now - with the sasquatch asleep it wouldn't see them coming anyways.

Brandishing the sporting rifle in one hand and Callahan's GPS tracker in the other, Tom motioned ahead of him as if to say "this way". They would need to stay absolutely silent to avoid waking the beast. Isabel and

Callahan followed him in single file along the southern edge of the ravine. Lifting their feet as they walked and treading as lightly as possible in order to make the least amount of noise, they watched the ravine floor below them for any sign of the hiding monster.

As they reached the corner in the gully where Harmony had been found, Tom paused to take a moment of silence. Callahan understood the significance, and placed a hand on Tom's shoulder. Tom looked him in the eye and Callahan nodded, as if to say *this is why we're here. Let's get the son of a bitch.* Tom breathed in a deep sigh, and continued marching northeast up the ravine.

Now the "sasquatch" dot on the GPS and the dot that marked their current location was growing closer, and the map began to zoom in so that Tom could get a better look of where exactly the sasquatch was. It was about a hundred yards up ahead, around a gentle curve in the ravine and right out of their sight, resting against the northern wall. *Perfect,* Tom thought. *We'll have a perfect shot.* He looked at the other two and pantomimed a zipper across his lips. *We're getting close now, dead silence.*

The birds chirped in the trees above them and squirrels played around in the understory, allowing them some sonic cover to conceal the sounds of their breath and footsteps across the forest floor. The wind blew gently now off the mountain to the north, so they could stay downwind from the sasquatch. The sun was shining, evaporating the fog away from the mountainside. The weather was perfect.

Rounding the corner, they came across a bluff that separated the walkable trail from the gully's rim, driving them ten or twenty feet further from the beast and putting up a stone-and-earth outcrop of cover ten or fifteen feet tall for them. The GPS indicated that the beast was asleep right on the other side of the earthen wall. Tom signalled for the others to stay back, and with the AR-15 went ahead a few dozen yards to where the earthen wall ended to get a sneak peek.

Peeking around the bluff, Tom was confused by what he saw. The ravine opened up into a gentle curve again, and the rocky outcropping on the other side, some twelve feet tall here, dug into the earth to create a little grotto. It looked exactly like where Tom expected a great ape to set up its home, but there was no sasquatch. Confused, he turned back to Callahan and Isabel and mouthed the words, “It's not here!”

“What?” Callahan mouthed back.

“It's! Not! Here!” He responded silently, more slowly this time.

“What do you mean it's not here?” Callahan whispered this time.

Tom held up a finger to his lip, reminding the old man to be silent. “I don't know,” he mouthed, “but it's not here. I'm going down to check.”

“No, no, no!” Callahan and Isabel both mouthed at the same time, but it was too late. Tom was over the lip of the ravine and was carefully walking down the slope like a mountain-goat, being doubly careful to neither lose his footing or disturb anything that would make sound.

“Stupid son-of-a-bitch,” Callahan muttered. Isabel shot him an offended look, but he shook it off. “Come on!” he motioned, and advanced to the edge of the bluff where he could see what Tom was doing. Isabel followed closely behind, clutching her rifle.

Tom was halfway down the side of the ravine now, not even looking back at his compatriots. He gingerly dismounted the wall, still being as graceful as possible to not make a noise, and crossed the three yards across the ravine floor to where the GPS locator was supposed to be. Checking the sat-phone, he peered into the detritus on the ravine floor before plunging down into it. He picked up a small round pill-shaped object with a pulsing LED inside it, still attached to bits of sinew, dried blood, and orange hair.

"God fucking damnit," he swore out loud. The tracker had fallen out of the sasquatch. He turned around to show it to the other two. "It's not in the sasquatch anymore," he hissed. "Who knows where it is?"

Suddenly, Tom's eyes grew wide. He froze in place in terror, unable to lift his gun and shoot as a large, greyish-black hand clutched the edge of the grotto entrance. Slowly, a shaggy head covered in long, orange hair emerged, two soulless eyes glowering at Tom. Then, its broad shoulders emerged, and then its stout body and long legs. The creature was bigger than Tom remembered, standing at least eight feet tall and four hundred pounds. It wiped the sleep from its eyes and looked at him curiously, before its face contorted into one of rage. It inhaled, and let out a terrifying roar.

"Tom!" Isabel cried from atop the ridge. "Run!"

Tom couldn't move. He was petrified, literally frozen in place with fear. He gripped the AR-15 white-knuckled, unable to even raise it to defend itself as the sasquatch sniffed the air around it and took an ambling step towards him. Up on the ridge, Isabel screamed and raised the twenty-two, firing off four shots. They seemed to bounce off the sasquatch, not doing it any harm. The beast howled furiously, and stooped down onto its knuckles to charge him.

A rock flew out of the cave entrance behind the sasquatch and struck it on the back, taking it by surprise. It grunted in confusion and turned its back on Tom, spotting Isabel up on the ridge. The creature's eyes no longer on him, Tom found himself freed from his trance. He raised the AR-15 and opened fire, screaming with each burst of rounds, "Die, motherfucker! Die! Die, motherfucker, die! Die, motherfucker, die!" Four bursts of three rounds each exploded off the ravine wall and floor around the sasquatch, with two rounds grazing the beast.

The beast turned back towards him and lurched at him again. This time, he didn't freeze up. He raised the rifle again, aiming for the creature's head, and squeezed the trigger as fast as he could. Ten rounds fired. Six went over the sasquatch, missing it entirely and embedding themselves in the ravine wall. Two grazed the Sasquatch's shoulder, ultimately also striking the earth behind it. But two rounds fired true, and struck the beast in the chest and neck. Stumbling backwards, the sasquatch fell to the ravine floor, allowing Tom to see the cave entrance behind it.

Jason, bloodied and battered, peeked into the daylight, clutching a baseball-sized rock in his fist. He threw the rock down onto the sasquatch and gingerly stepped over its motionless form, limping as fast as he could to rejoin his brother.

"Jason!" Tom cried. "You're alive!"

"Where's Elise?" Jason croaked hoarsely, sitting against the edge of the ravine and wiping a mixture of dried blood and mud from his forehead. "Is she okay?"

"Elise is fine," Tom said, dropping the rifle and embracing his brother. "Callahan had her airlifted out of here."

He gestured up onto the ridge behind Jason, where Callahan waved.

"Holy shit, *the* Callahan? Sheriff Callahan? How are you doing, old man? You must be ninety by now!" Jason cried.

Callahan and Isabel started to make their way down the ravine to join the reunion. "Hardly ninety," Callahan said. "Try seventy-seven!"

Jason laughed. "Well you look incredible! Whatever you're doing, it's working."

Isabel threw her arms around him. "We were so worried about you!" She said, "We thought that the sasquatch, you know, killed you!"

"I thought so, too," replied Jason. "Until I woke up to the sound of gunfire just now. He hit my head pretty hard."

"We're glad to see you're okay," Callahan said, reaching a hand out for Jason to shake. "These sasquatches, they don't usually kill people, but they're wild animals. Just like a problem bear, sometimes you get one that you just gotta take out."

"Uh, Sheriff," Tom said, pointing over his shoulder, "about that."

Callahan turned around and saw the sasquatch, groaning in pain, picking itself up off the ground. Suddenly, he realized that they had sacrificed their vantage point and were now on a level playing field with the beast who had just seemed to have eaten thirty bullets without dying. "Oh no," he said, "oh no no no, this isn't good. Run!"

The sasquatch bellowed its war-cry once again, and dropped to all fours and began to charge. Jason and Isabel ran to the right, Tom ran to the left, but Callahan stayed put.

"Andrew!" Tom yelled. "What are you doing?"

"Run!" Callahan repeated.

The sasquatch quickly closed the distance to Callahan and rose to its full height, scooped him up off the ground like a rag-doll. Tom ran about fifty feet then tripped in the leaf litter, turning back to watch with horror as the beast shook the old man in its massive hands. "Callahan!" Tom cried.

"Remember," Callahan yelled after him, "it's not every sasquatch! Just the problem ones that gotta be pruned!" As the sasquatch gripped his legs in its other hand, he reached into his coat-pocket and produced a small green item the size and shape of a baseball.

The fragmentation grenade.

"No, no, no!" Tom yelled.

"I'll tell your dad you said hi," he smirked. The old man pulled the pin and shouted "Hit the dirt!"

The sasquatch roared with rage and tore Andrew Callahan in half at the waist. Callahan let out a haunting scream which faded into a gurgling moan as his legs went limp. His upper body, leaking blood and intestines, seemed to seize for a second, a grin creeping across his face, as his arm rolled limply downwards and his grip loosened, and released the grenade.

Isabel, Jason, and Tom all dove face-first into the dirt and covered their ears as a blast rocked the forest, raining them in dirt, leaves, red chunks of meat, and orange hair. The roar was deafening, but the silence that followed was even moreso. The explosion echoed off the mountains around them and faded into a silence no bird dared break. Slowly, Tom rose to his feet and turned around to face where his friend, Andrew Callahan, had last stood. Nothing remained but a crater of blood and upturned soil in the bottom of the ravine.

The sasquatch was dead. Harmony Carlini had been avenged.

## Chapter Seventeen

"Tom," Dr. Meyer said, "you can't really expect me to believe this whole story. You know that, right?"

"It's true," Tom responded, "every single word of it."

The therapist sighed and rubbed the bridge of her nose. "Tom, I can't help you if you're not going to tell me the truth. No sasquatch, no heroic last stand with a hand-grenade, just tell me what's bothering you."

"Doc, I'm telling you exactly what happened. You can take my word for it or not. I've even started writing a book about it."

Dr. Meyer checked her watch. "Look, we're out of time for today. Tom? If you're not going to be honest with me, I don't think I can continue working with you, so I'm not scheduling you for next week. Listen, please find yourself a new therapist and tell them the truth. You need it."

Tom rolled his eyes. "Okay, Dr. Meyer. It's been nice getting to know you."

"You too, Tom," she said, and disconnected the video call.

It had been a month since Tom had returned from Alaska, and what a month it had been. Alice had been discharged from hospice, and had moved to Kansas City to stay in Tom and Isabel's guest bedroom. His girls didn't really understand what all had happened, and had gone back to school after spring break like nothing had changed. Jason and Elise were both hospitalized together in Anchorage until they were stable enough to leave, then went back to Texas, but last time Tom had talked to Jason, he had said that he was planning on moving back to Alaska. Without the Sasquatch out there, he felt safe enough to move back onto the family property and raise his own children there, giving them the childhood that he had always wanted.

Tom stood up from his computer in his new makeshift office in the living room and stretched, then mounted the stairs up to his old office which was now Alice's bedroom. He politely knocked on the door. "Mom?" He asked. "You doing okay?"

"Mmhmm!" Alice responded. "Just getting ready for bed, dear!"

"Mom, it's three in the afternoon."

"Did I say bed? I meant nap. Going down for a nap."

Tom chuckled. He was glad that his mom was doing better for sure, but living with her again was an adjustment. He crossed the hall to his bedroom, where Isabel was changing out of her work clothes. Knocking on the door, he asked, "Hey Isa, can I come in?"

"Of course," she replied.

Tom pushed the door open and entered the bedroom, closing it behind him. Sitting down on the bed, he asked her, "Can I ask you something I've been thinking about?"

Isabel pulled on a clean t-shirt. "What is it, Tom?"

"Jason wants to move out to the property. Now that it's safe and all."

"Right," she said, sitting beside him.

"And I was kind of thinking, why not, you know?"

"Why not what, Tom?"

"Why not move back? Go live on the mountain, like dad wanted for us in the first place? We can build a second house on the property. There's plenty of room and we've got the money. Give the girls what I was supposed to have as a kid. We'd talk it over with them first, of course, and with Jace and Elise. And with mom. I'm sure she'd love it. She loves it out there."

Isabel mulled it over. "And then, when the time comes for Alice to go…"

"Exactly," Tom said. "Dad and Harmony are already out there. It would be perfect. And we don't have enough to keep both properties, and I would hate to sell it when mom's estate runs out of money."

Isabel kissed Tom on the cheek. "We'll talk it over, okay?"

"Promise?"

"Promise."

---

Tom's silver SUV took the right-hand turn at Talkeetna and left the pavement to officially enter the dirt roads of the forest. There was no suspense in the air this time. The woods were safe and wonderful and full of life, and to Tom Carlini it was like he was seeing it for the first time. The girls were in the back seat, looking out the window at all the trees passing by, and Isabel kept pointing out wildlife that they saw. "Look, a deer! Look, girls! A rabbit!" Tom smiled. This was the forest he remembered.

The truck made a right turn onto the gravel driveway at the old weathered mailbox labeled "CARLINI" in faded white letters. That would need to be touched up, of course. About a hundred feet down the driveway, though, it now split off in three directions. Tom turned right. They could drop Alice, who was asleep in the backseat with the girls, off at her house afterwards. The girls were too eager to see their new home. Another quarter mile down a freshly built gravel driveway, the SUV entered a clearing where a newly constructed two-story contemporary cabin-style house stood. "This is it, girls," Tom said, pulling into the yard so they could get a clear view out of the left-hand windows. "Welcome to paradise!"

The girls flung open the door and ran into the yard with a chorus of "oohs" and "ahs". Tom smiled at his wife, took her hand, and said, "Let's let them in to explore, shall we?" The adults climbed out of the truck and Tom handed the key to Isabel, who called the girls to the porch so she could show them the house. Tom rounded the truck and opened the right-side back door to help his mother out.

"Where are we, Tom?" Alice asked.

Tom looked up at the treeline and smiled. "We're home, mom."

---

A memorial service was held for Andrew Callahan, and much to Tom's surprise, most of the town of Skitooa turned out to see him off, as well as well-wishers from Talkeetna, Sitna, and as far as Wasilla. Tom offered to host the ceremony on his property, but it was held at the church downtown instead. The Carlinis were all in attendance, with Tom, Isa, Alice, Nat, and Emma Lee riding in Tom's SUV and Jason, Elise, and Butler in Jason's brand new pickup truck. It was a touching service, and though Tom wanted to speak on the bravery of the Andrew Callahan he knew, he also knew it was Callahan's wish that the existence of the sasquatch be kept a secret - for now at least - to protect the majority of the creatures which weren't monsters. Jason was called upon to speak his memories of Callahan, and he simply called him an honorable man who served his community well both in and out of uniform, and a lifelong friend of his fathers and therefore of all the Carlinis.

After the service, Tom loaded his wife, kids, and mother back into his truck and they headed back out into the woods. The SUV handled the bumpy double-track road fairly well, and it was a comfortable enough ride that the children, tired as they were, drifted off to sleep. Tom and Isabel weren't in much of a talking mood, and they drove along in silence with the windows down so they could listen to the sound of music.

Something jumped out into the road, and Tom braked suddenly, waking everyone from their sleep. The deer stared Tom dead in the eye for a second, then finished crossing the road safely. Tom turned to Isabel and said, "I love the wildlife out here."

Isabel's face changed to one of horror for just a second, then the horror changed to amazement. She pointed out the windshield and whispered, "Tom! Kids! Look!"

About ten yards in front of the truck, a golden-haired sasquatch stepped out into the roadway. She was a female, about six feet tall. She made eye contact with Tom and he was surprised to see that her eyes were gentle, kind, and almost human. She looked the SUV up and down, assessing whether it posed a threat, and, once she had decided that it was safe, turned back towards the forest behind her and let out a sort of low whistling sound. To the amazement of everyone in the vehicle, a second sasquatch emerged, this one young and around three feet tall. His arms waved lankily by his knees as he wandered out into the roadway. He turned and looked at the truck as well, and his face mirrored the amazement that everyone in the vehicle felt at the sight. Then his mother reached behind him and gently guided him across the road with her massive hand. She turned to look at the SUV one more time, with a mixture of curiosity and caution, then disappeared with her young one into the undergrowth.

Tom turned to his family and asked "Did you see that?"

Isabel held out her phone to show Tom. "I did. I got a video, too!"

Tom watched the video in amazement. Here was verifiable proof that these creatures existed, which the scientific community would go berserk over. He took the phone from Isa and watched the video twice over.

Then, the words of Andrew Callahan came back to his mind. These were peaceful creatures, who lived in isolation and secrecy for thousands of years. The Monster had been an anomaly. Most of them were more scared of humans than humans were of them. "Isa," he said, handing the phone back to her, "you know you have to delete this video, right?"

Isabel sighed. "You're right." She swiped up on her phone and hit the 'delete' button. "They're our neighbors. We can't let them be exploited. They have to stay our little secret."

Tom nodded, "For Callahan."

"For Callahan."

Tom smiled at his wife, then turned back forward and pressed down on the accelerator. The truck continued on its way down the double-track road towards the Carlini Property.

## Epilogue

Alice Carlini passed away in her sleep surrounded by friends and family during the summer of 2020, living in Paradise until her last day. It was true that she had gotten better before passing, and she was able to sit on the porch and enjoy the Alaskan mountains that her husband had loved so much. She was buried alongside him and their daughter, Harmony, on the family plot.

Tom and Isabel had a third child in 2021, whom they named Alice after her late grandmother. They, and all three of their girls, remain on the Carlini Property to this day. Tom is working on instilling his daughters with as much of a love for nature as his father instilled in him.

Jason, Elise, and their son Butler remain on the property as well. Elise's hearing in the damaged ear never returned, but she was able to get much of her ear surgically rebuilt. She now wears her hair long to hide the scar.

The summer after Callahan sacrificed himself to save them, Tom and Elise took the girls down to the ravine to the location of the final showdown between the family and the monster, near where Harmony's remains had been found thirty years prior. They built a secret little stone memorial to Callahan there in the forest, which stands to this day.

The new sasquatches who moved into the area proved friendly. Since the Carlinis no longer keep chickens, they no longer have to worry about egg theft. They often leave out offerings of nuts, berries, and dried fruit for the sasquatches, which the apes readily accept. In return, the creatures often leave pinecones, small shiny objects, bits of string, and all manner of other trinkets that they find as payment. On summer nights, the Carlinis sit on the porch and listen to the sasquatches calling to each other in the woods. They are learning to identify them by their voices, and naming the different individuals. Occasionally, they'll come right up to the edge of the woods and whistle, but they never emerge into the clearing, and they never make the Carlinis feel unsafe. Quite the opposite, actually.

Tom ended up writing a book about his encounters, but eventually decided not to publish it. It's what Callahan would have wanted. The sasquatches remain their little secret to this day. Instead, Tom and Jason put their love of fantasy together and wrote a fantasy novel about a little girl who discovers a secret kingdom in the woods behind her house. They published the novel in the autumn of 2021, and dedicated it to the memory of their little sister, Harmony. The book is titled “Harm’s Queendom”.

Tom is also working on compiling a book about the creatures which will be marketed as fiction. He is dedicating it to Callahan’s memory, and entitling it “An Amateur’s Field Guide To The Sasquatch”. He will stress repeatedly in the book that it is a work of fiction.

## Acknowledgements

This book would not have been possible without the help of several people, so I'd like to acknowledge and thank the following:

Thanks to **my Papa**, who advised me on wild animals and guns and whatnot, and to whom this book is dedicated.

Thanks to **my mom**, **Cody VanAlst**, **Silver Roman**, **Jeff Chitty**, and **M. N. Jolley**, who read my early drafts and helped me with editing and catching my plot-holes.

Thanks to **the users of r/bigfoot on Reddit,** who helped me figure out my hypothetical sasquatch anatomy and biology so I could treat the beast as a real living animal.

Thanks to **Professor Jeff Meldrum for his scientific research on the sasquatch phenomenon, from which I borrowed indiscriminately.**

Thanks to **Makinzie Knox** and Holoframe Publishing, LLC for helping polish this book and getting it published for me.

Finally, thanks to **you, the reader** for making it this far. I hope you enjoyed, and I hope you pick up the next one I write, too.

www.ingramcontent.com/pod-product-compliance
Ingram Content Group UK Ltd.
Pitfield, Milton Keynes, MK11 3LW, UK
UKHW021650190726
13853UKWH00001B/168

9 798330 493425